THE

CHALLENGE

JOY BACH

How many stories do you have hidden inside? I challenge you to get those thoughts on paper. Give your loved ones a chance to take a peek at them.

ISBN 978-0-9994956-4-3

Kudos to FaithWriters

My emergence as a writer was tentative. Could I really write? Who would read it? The questions swirled. Somewhere along that journey I stumbled upon a website called *FaithWriters*. Their spiel described them as a safe place to learn and grow in my writing ability.

Was I ready for that?

I joined in 2007…and I've never been the same since. Almost weekly a topic was assigned, and we were to write about it in 750 words or less. Imagine my surprise when I regularly went over that limit.

Where were these words coming from?

I am forever grateful for the nudging I received, the critiques that were given and the encouragement bestowed on me as I progressed. After attending some of their conferences, I met and maintain friendships with some remarkable people.

Who knew the *FaithWriters* path would lead to my own blog website and the publication of two books…and counting, as this is book three.

Meet Joy Bach

Joy Bach was married for 35 years to John, a wonderful man who has now graduated from this life's school.

Joy is a mom and grandma who loves to read, write, crochet, knit, travel and spend time with family and friends. She finally retired at the end of 2017.

Her articles have appeared on the FaithWriters and Jewels of Encouragement websites and in Called magazine. Her first book, Life Moments with Joy, was published on December 5, 2017, giving her a wonderful 75th birthday present. Then, for her 77th birthday, book number two was published, More Life Moments with Joy.

Over the years, Joy has helped organize and lead singles' groups, taught classes for women, spoken at retreats and been instrumental in starting a Celebrate Recovery group at her church.

Joy's newest endeavor is the creation of a group called Life after Loss. As a recent widow, she became aware of the need for support for women struggling to figure out their place in life after the loss of their spouse. The gathering meets once a week in her home where they discuss everything from how to pay bills to cooking for one. The camaraderie is uplifting and encouraging.

For more of Joy's articles or to contact her, visit her website at:
thewordsbydesign.com

I had no idea the impact Joy would have on my life. She is one of the strongest women I know. Her strength, courage, empathy, compassion, curiosity, and most of all the love I have gained from her is empowering. I have been incredibly lucky that G-d and my grandparents sent her to me. I am sure I can speak for most people she comes in contact with to say she is a wonderful example of what faith and determination demonstrates in the face of adversity.

I will never forget what she said to me several years ago when she asked me to come and stay with her and her husband. "Come stay with us. I will need you in six months to a year". Well, she has certainly filled that hole in my heart where my grandparents resided.

Thank you,

Trigg Bell
Daughter from another mother

Contents

Topic: Fearful | **Release from Fear** — 13

Topic: Emotionally Bold | **A Big Dream** — 16

Topic: Surprised | **Intersections** — 19

Topic: Calm | **Choosing Sanity** — 22

Topic: Fellowship | **Friends Forever** — 25

Topic: Christian Baptism | **My Identification** — 28

Topic: Sunday School | **Polly** — 30

Topic: Evangelism | **Notches in Your Belt** — 32

Topic: Encouragement | **Does Your Wife Have a Name?** — 35

Topic: At the Pulpit | **The Peanut Butter Jar** — 38

Topic: Gifts of the Spirit or Service | **Gift or Burden** — 41

Topic: Home Group | **Extended Family** — 43

Topic: The Church | **Worldwide Access** — 46

Topic: A Stitch in Time Saves Nine | **Expectations** — 49

Topic: A Bird in the Hand is Worth Two in the Bush | **The Real Thing** — 52

Topic: Don't Try to Walk Before You Can Crawl | **Cart Before the Horse** — 55

Topic: All that Glitters is Not Gold | **The Proposition** — 58

Topic: A Man is Known by the Company He Keeps | **Starbucks Gang** — 60

Topic: It's No Use Crying Over Spilt Milk | **No Do-Overs** — 63

Topic: Don't Cut Off Your Nose to Spite Your Face | **Groceries and Hats** — 66

Topic: Actions Speak Louder than Words | **Forgiving Mother** — 69

Topic: Every Dark Cloud has a Silver Lining | **Cancer and Trust** — 72

Topic: Make Hay While the Sun Shines | **The Yellow Bowl** — 75

Topic: Grandparents | **The Saga of Marie** — 78

Topic: Mother (as in maternal parent) | **Honor Thy Mother** — 81

Topic: Siblings | **My Haven** — 84

Topic: In-Laws | **Popo and Nana** — 87

Topic: The Family Pet | **Emotional Roller Coaster** — 90

Topic: Cousins | **Imposter in the Midst** — 93

Topic: The Family Home | **Where's Your Heart?** — 95

Topic: The Family Reunion | **Thanks for the Memories** — 98

Topic: Telephone | **Texting Queen** — 101

Topic: Concentration | **Simplifying** — 104

Topic: Hide and Seek | **The Consequence** — 107

Topic: Charade | **The Good Wife** — 110

Topic: Snap | **The Wisdom of Mac** — 113

Topic: The Game of Life | **The Breath of Life** — 116

Topic: Christmas Tree | **Bethlehem Village** — 119

Topic: Christmas Cooking/Baking | **Traditions Old and New** — 122

Topic: Countdown to Christmas/Advent | **Is It Christmas Yet?** — 125

Topic: Christmas Lights | **Inner Joy** — 128

Topic: Christmas Cards | **The Personal Touch** — 131

Topic: Christmas Gifts | **It's the Thought That Counts** — 134

Topic: The Reason for the Season of Christmas | **I Have Jesus** — 137

Topic: The USA | **Capturing the Spirit** — 140

Topic: The United Kingdom | **Blimey…and More** — 143

Topic: Canada | **A Lovely Neighbor** — 146

Topic: Europe | **Bathroom Adventures** — 149

Topic: The Kingdom of God | **Stronghold of Protection** — 152

Topic: Up and Down | **Being Normal** — 155

Topic: Hot and Cold | **Motorcycles and Blankets** — 158

Topic: Beginning and End | **The Cycle of Life** — 161

Topic: Hard and Soft | **Concrete and Sponges** — 162

Topic: In and Out | **Pattern Choices** — 166

Topic: Light and Dark | **Invisible Boundaries** — 169

Topic: Bitter and Sweet | **Role Models** — 172

Topic: Empty and Full | **Now You See It, | Now You Don't** — 175

Topic: Twilight Years of Life | **The Waiting Place** — 177

Topic: Summer | **Imitating the Cheshire Cat** — 180

Topic: Adolescence/Teen Years | **Life in the Blender** — 183

Topic: Spring (the season) | **Tornado Alley** — 186

Topic: Winter (the season) | **Who Moved** — 189

Topic: Birth (infancy) | **Inadequate Instructions** — 192

Topic: Childhood | **The Schism in my World** — 194

Topic: Ow! | **A Three-Letter Word** — 197

Topic: Oops | **Who Knew** — 199

Topic: Huh? | **Motorcycle Moments** — 201

Topic: Grrr! | **Road Rage** — 204

Topic: Phew! | **The Long Slide** — 207

Topic: Shhh | **Secrets** — 209

Topic: Inspiration/Block (for the writer) | **Words in a Book** — 212

Topic: Book Store/Library | **Choices** — 214

Topic: Hear | **The Art of Listening** — 216

Topic: Taste | **Taste of Freedom** — 219

Topic: Feel (Emotions) | **Change of Address** — 222

Topic: Think | **Conversations with Myself** — 225

Topic: The Inner Person | **Masks of Many Designs** — 228

Topic: Writing a Letter (handwritten correspondence) | **My Gift to You**   **231**

Topic: Gossip/Rumors | **Dan and Ernie**   **234**

Topic: Billboard/Poster/Sign | **Roadside Reading**   **236**

Topic: Foreign Language | **Outsider in Our Midst**   **238**

Topic: Communication Breakdown | **Say What?**   **240**

Topic: Seasons of a Year or Life | **The World from Alta's View**   **242**

Topic: Year(s) | **Oh My, What a Year**   **245**

Topic: 24 Hours | **Time With the Healer**   **248**

Topic: Era | **The Silent Generation**   **251**

Topic: Week(s) | **So Many Memories**   **254**

Topic: Time-Consuming | **24 Hours**   **257**

Topic: Handout | **Giver or Receiver**   **259**

Topic: Outstanding | **Musician Extraordinaire**   **262**

Topic: Don't Look Back | **Banishing the Ogre**   **265**

Topic: Weary | **Burnout**   **267**

Topic: Risk | **The First Step is the Hardest**   **270**

Topic: Hum | **What is that Sound**   **273**

Topic: Expose | **I Am Woman**   **275**

Topic: Like a Fish Out of Water | **English as a Second Language**   **277**

Topic: Count Your Blessings | **Connections**   **279**

More books by Joy Bach

Life Moments with Joy
More Life Moments with Joy

Release from Fear

Growing up in the "Bible Belt", I knew my place as wife; especially as a preacher's wife. My duties were to keep the house clean, cook the meals, watch after the children and do everything perfectly. I was to be "seen" and not "heard". My place was in the house; no job and no friends. Three children and 11 years of marriage later, I had my role down to a science.

And then my husband left.

Life became a struggle; financially, emotionally and physically. We were living on welfare (as I had no job skills). As mortifying as that was, the shame was compounded by my church asking me to leave the membership. The philosophy given me was that if my husband left me, there must be something wrong with me.

I was slowly selling the beautiful pieces of furniture in the nine-room house that had his name on the lease. I had no idea what my husband's plans were. But I knew what my job was; to keep us together until he came back.

I existed through the days, making money as a babysitter, seamstress and housecleaner. And I waited.

It was a summer Saturday. Busy around the house, I had my hair in curlers. My housedress was orange and it just hung on me. My weight had dropped to 104.

The doorbell rang. I never had company. Cautiously I opened the door and there stood my brother, Bob. He had married and moved away when I was four years old, so our relationship was not a really close one. He lived in Colorado and I lived in Nebraska. And now he stood at my door. What could he want?

I invited him in, but he declined, saying, "Let's just sit here on the porch in this glider". He quieted my questions with a wave of his hand and said, "I'm here for one thing and one thing only. I want to see the whites of your eyes while I talk with you". I felt the impact of his words in my stomach. What had I done to him?

He began to bombard me with questions. "Why are you still married? What are you going to do with your life? Why don't you have a job?" As I tried to answer him, I noticed I had the same three answers for everything. "The church won't let me. Mother said I couldn't." Or, "What would people think?"

I had a life-long history of not being allowed to think for myself. And now Bob expected me to have some answers. The more he questioned, the sicker I became. After about two hours, I began to cry.

"What do you want from me?" I asked him.

"When I hear the answer I'm looking for, I will leave" was his reply.

But he changed his direction with the questions.

"Do you think you're smart?"

"I know I am. I got straight A's in high school."

"Do you like the way you are living now?"

No one had ever asked me that. And I certainly had never voiced any commentary on my life. The church had arranged our marriage because they felt I would be the best preacher's wife (I was 17 at the time). Who was I to argue? But deep inside I felt life could be better.

"No, I don't really like this" I answered. But my body began to tremble. My mother's religion had me condemned to hell if I took the initiative and took charge of my life.

"What do you think you can do to change it?" Bob continued.

Timidly, in fear of being struck by lightening, I said, "I could get a divorce and start over somewhere else".

Bob stood up.

"Where are you going?"

"Home" he said. "I got the answer I came for", and he did, indeed, turn around and drive back to Colorado.

He gave me a chance at life that day and I took it. Scary? You bet. Hard? Yes. But I discovered I am a very strong woman and have many creative abilities.

I now know that Bob did a very hard thing. He knew how he was scaring me. But he was teaching me to think for myself. He helped me see that I had the right to make a life for the girls and me. He knew how I had been raised. It took "tough love" to break through to the real me.

A Big Dream

In 1992, I had a conversation with a friend, Don. After hearing about a big dream I believed God had given me about reaching women who had been wounded by life, as I had, he invited me to Toastmasters. I asked what Toastmasters was. When I heard that a group of people sat around and listened as members took turns speaking and then someone would evaluate that speech in front of everyone, I knew I could never go there.

Over the next six years, I allowed myself to occasionally consider Don's suggestion. I stood at a fork in the road. On one side was my "Comfort Zone" and on the other was my "Big Dream". When my palms grew sweaty and my breath came in gulps, I thought about something else. NO WAY COULD I GET UP IN FRONT OF PEOPLE AND THEN OPEN MY MOUTH AND HAVE WORDS COME OUT!!! I chose comfort.

But God would not let me go. I began to understand it was time to leave this "Comfort Zone".

One Thursday in April of 1998, I drove cautiously by the Toastmaster's meeting place. No harm came to me. But what would happen when I attended the meeting there the next morning?

I quietly gathered my clothes and crept from the bedroom at 5:00 a.m. Tears filled my eyes as I headed out through the dark in my car. But friendly people greeted me. I searched for Don. He was not there. I knew I would have to hurt him. Didn't he know this was the morning I would show up after six years!!!

I joined the club. In May of 1998, I was scheduled to give my ice breaker. Days before, I began to feel ill. My intestinal tract was rebelling.

There was no sleep for me that Thursday night. I cried as I dressed. I cried as I drove. I argued with myself. "Why are you doing this? Are you crazy?" But I kept going. My "Big Dream" was calling.

I did it. I spoke five minutes in front of people and words actually came out of my mouth.

It took six speeches for my terror to lessen. I no longer cried and ran to the bathroom. My heart just pounded out of my chest and my face turned beet red. No problem! I was improving.

In July of 1999, I began working on the Storytelling Manual and discovered that was my style of speaking. I could tell stories! By January of 2000 my heart was better and the redness in my face no longer competed with Rudolph.

Then came that Saturday when I competed in the Division Contest. About a minute into the speech, I opened my mouth, and nothing came out. And nothing came out. And nothing came out. I know exactly how long nothing came out, because another Toastmaster was there with a tape recorder. He later timed the silence and told me.

Do you have any idea how long one minute and 14 seconds are when you are standing in front of a group of people and they are expecting you to say something? I had faced my greatest fear and did not run crying from the room. I completed the speech. And I was still alive!

Over the next three years I calmed down enough to notice that there were actually people in front of me, listening. I was getting the hang of it.

I stepped way out of my "Comfort Zone" by conducting a "Success and Leadership" module at our Advanced Toastmaster Club. For 63 minutes, I stood in front of the room with words coming out of my mouth. I'm sure it was not a momentous night for the attendees. But I could not go to sleep that night. I kept saying to my husband, "I did it".

Each level of achievement brings me one step closer to my "Big Dream".

Great opportunities await you and me, if we are willing to take the risks. We need to dream big, using God's imagination. Another "Big Dream" is out there waiting for us.

If we don't pursue it, that something important will never happen.

Intersections

I grew up in a town where we had city blocks. Therefore, we had intersections. Today our streets are meandering and can go for blocks without an intersection.

Life has intersections too. Some of us feel like we live in a life that has an intersection every block and some of us have a life of meandering before we get to that intersection. But we all have them.

I reached my very first intersection when I was just a few hours old. I didn't know I had reached one, but with the death of my father, the life I would have lived was forever changed. Suddenly our little family had no income, and I was raised in a household that struggled to have enough food.

When I was 15, I found myself at another huge intersection. My church decided that I would marry the preacher's son. I never dated. He and I attended church together. And then we married while I was still in high school.

When I was 30, I arrived at an intersection that had been invisible around the bend. My husband suddenly left us. I had no job, no money and three children.

Are you thinking of some of the intersections in your life? You cannot go on a journey without coming to intersections.

The Bible tells of a man who reached a huge intersection and his life was forever changed. In Acts, it tells us that Saul had been an official witness in Jerusalem at the stoning of Stephen. He had heard Stephen's last words when he prayed, "Lord, don't charge them with this sin." It must have infuriated Saul, because he went from house to house, dragging out both men and women to throw them into jail.

He was so eager to destroy the Lord's followers that he went to the high priest and requested letters addressed to the synagogues in Damascus, asking their cooperation in the arrest of any followers he found there. He was willing to walk 150 miles to complete this undertaking!!!

Saul was traveling down the road from Jerusalem to Damascus, intent on carrying out his plans. Suddenly, he came to a huge intersection!

A blinding light from heaven shone down on him and he fell to the ground. And then he heard a voice. The men that were traveling with Saul were speechless. They heard a voice but saw no one. They were at an intersection of their own. Saul had been blinded and had to be led by his companions into Damascus.

Let's leave that intersection and go across town to a different one. The Lord was telling a man named Ananias to go visit Saul. Ananias knew who Saul was. He knew Saul's agenda.

Ananias stood at an intersection. What if he hadn't taken that walk across town to visit Saul?

What kind of intersection are you facing? Will you continue going straight? Or will you make that turn and change your life forever?

Saul became a preacher. Talk about a drastic change. So much so that even his name changed. He became Paul.

No matter your age, you will still come to intersections.

One day I spoke in my daughter's middle school Speech class. Sitting in the front row was a girl with horrible scars running down her cheeks. She had been scalped when her hair was caught in a piece of machinery. It had pulled the skin from her face. She had reached a huge intersection in her life!

My topic that day was "intersections". She understood.

One boy talked about the intersection his uncle had reached when he had gone hunting with a friend and the friend had been accidentally shot. His uncle held his friend while he died. That intersection caused him to become an alcoholic.

Last weekend, I helped move a lady from an apartment to her daughter's house. This lady is in her 80's and has reached a huge intersection in her life. She has always been very independent. And now she no longer has a spot that is just hers. It's not an easy intersection.

Think about the intersections in your life. How well are you handling them?

No matter how huge your intersection, you can make it safely through if you keep your focus on Jesus. He will take that turn with you and walk down the new path beside you. And if you get too weary or afraid, He will carry you in His arms, close to His chest.

Choosing Sanity

My world had shattered. In the space of six months, my sister, who had been like a mother to me, had died suddenly at the age of 42. My husband had unexpectedly left. And his father, the only dad I had ever known, informed me on the telephone that they never wanted to see or hear from me again. My mother's comforting words were, "What did you do to him, to make him leave?"

Alone.

I had no job, no skills, no friends, no money and the list went on. I was terrified. My husband had been in total control of everything. Now I was in charge. One choice I pondered was to let go of my mind and just let them lock me away where someone else would take care of me. That was the easy way out.

But what would happen to my children? Tough as it was, I would have to choose sanity.

Having been raised in the church, I knew God was there somewhere. I wasn't sure He cared about my situation. Night after night, I lay awake, terrified of the future and getting zero sleep. I knew my body could not continue to function this way. If I continued handling my circumstances with panic, the girls would soon have neither father nor mother. So, I searched for a way out of this torment.

One night as I lay wide-eyed, God gently began to speak. When I tried to take over the conversation, I felt tenderly reproached and knew it was my turn to listen. But I had SO much to say.

Gradually my spirit calmed. Slowly new realizations and thoughts began to pop into my mind. I repeatedly asked of God. "How do I handle this over-whelming situation? How do I keep from panicking and being afraid?"

Through the dark night, God patiently explained letting go: relinquishment. What was accomplished by worrying all night? Did it make anything better? What was it doing to my relationship with my girls? The more He talked, the more I wanted to listen, agreeing with everything He said. But how could I change it? As the hours passed, my mind turned to scriptures memorized long ago; words very familiar to me yet suddenly acquiring a whole new meaning.

Early morning and still the lessons came. Instructions on how to sleep peace-fully. I listened with many doubts in my mind. Me, sleep peacefully? Perhaps with a shot from the doctor.

Yet very clearly the picture came to me; Jesus sitting on a hillside speaking lovingly to the people gathered to hear Him, compassion and tenderness on His face. I was sitting at His feet drinking in the words my weary emotions were so thirsty for. As I listened, I felt the anxiety lifting, the fears dissipating. Calmness. Very clearly, I understood I was to envision this scene at bedtime.

The first streaks of dawn came through the window. Had I been awake all night? Was everything a dream? Yet the absolute peace I felt was very real.

Evening came, the girls bathed and in bed and I sat on the front porch think-ing over the new ideas given to me. Eager to see if "they" worked, I climbed the stairs to my bed.

Closing my eyes, I envisioned the hillside and Jesus and me. Soon my brain was swamped with the bills I needed to pay and the job I couldn't find. "It didn't work", I heard myself say. Jerking my mind back under control, I set the scene again; the hillside, Jesus, me. All too soon, I was looking at the bills again.

Over several nights I struggled with my worries, with keeping my mind focused. And slowly, ever so slowly, it began to work. I could control my thoughts.

Due to poor eyesight, I would leave my glasses on until just before I fell asleep in case I needed to see anything in a hurry. As my new-found visualization technique began to work, it soon became apparent I needed to remove my glasses <u>before</u> I lay down. I fell asleep too quickly to leave them on!

The journey that seemed so terrifying became one of amazement as the scripture in Jeremiah 29:11 became a reality for me. God did have a plan for my future, far better than I could ever imagine.

Friends Forever

The first impression I had of the lady in the doorway was of a deer in the headlights. Wide-eyed, she was looking around the room. That's when I met Mary. We were having our "Small Group Rally" in the church auditorium. Our small group table had filled, so I was headed to the side of the room to get another chair. I looked up to see a petite, wide-eyed woman standing in the doorway.

"May I help you?" I asked.

She was there to find a small group, so I invited her to come to our table. I moved people over and gave her the chair I had procured. As the evening progressed, we exchanged information. She wasn't sure her husband would be interested. "He likes things like motorcycles". We assured her so did several men in our group. She nodded. Maybe he would come then.

And that is how our friendship began.

She and Jack began attending our small group. She was like a sponge, soaking up new insights. She jumped right in with both feet, eager to learn and grow.

They shared about their teenage daughter, Jody. Such a troubled child. And her boyfriend; a bad influence. But they still prayed for him.

Soon I felt a connection with Mary. We could communicate with eye contact, a raised eyebrow, a gesture. She would call me with questions and concerns the day after our group had met. She was afraid she might have offended someone with her comments. Or she disagreed with a statement that had been made and wanted to work through it with me.

We laughed and prayed together on the phone.

My concept of a telephone call is "bottom line". I just don't enjoy talking on the phone. But one evening, Mary called me at home with an extra urgency in her voice. As I listened, what I was really hearing was a mother who felt like a failure. She hadn't done enough or had done it wrong. Tears began to flow. We talked for two hours. In the end, she understood she had done the best she knew how, and Jody was making choices that Mary would not make.

Mary and Jack asked for prayer about selling their home. It all went very quickly. Soon they found the perfect place. Mary was so excited to have the group Christmas party in their new home.

Our church held a ground-breaking on July 10th for an addition. My husband John and I sat and talked with Mary, Jack and Jody. I saw the pain and fear in Mary's eyes when Jody left to go with her boyfriend.

August 1st was a beautiful sunny day.

As a bookkeeper, the first of the month is always a long day at work for me. I worked straight through from 7:30 to 4:30. Hungry and eager to get home, I was a little dismayed when John asked me to leave again as soon as I got home. He had purchased a new bicycle and very kindly asked me to take him to the cycle shop so he could ride it home. We pulled out of our driveway just as the 5:00 news came on the radio. We heard the words "two females shot at 26th and S. Edison". When John asked where 26th and Edison was, my answer was "Mary and Jack's".

I sat in the car in front of the cycle shop, while John went in to change into riding clothes. My cell phone rang. It was a lady from our "care group", asking me if I had heard about the shootings. She said they were showing Mary and Jack's house on television.

I told John the news update when he came out to the car to say I could go on home. By the time John got home, I had already called our Pastor. He and

John met at Mary and Jack's. Then John called to say they were following Jack to the Police Station. John's next phone call was the hardest. "The worst that could have happened has happened. They are both gone". Jack had been told his wife and daughter had been shot; murdered in their own home.

Mary and Jack were not at small group last night. But they were. We could see them, sitting on the couch, Mary's laugh echoing in the room. We have lost one of our family and we grieve. But not without hope. Mary has just moved again, sooner than she expected. Now she has a mansion.

And our phone calls have become a treasured memory.

My Identification

As a nine-year old, I had no idea what my mother was talking about when she explained that "next Sunday you are going to be baptized in the Cottonwood River". The river? But I couldn't swim. What if I didn't want to "be baptized"? No one asked.

The scene is still clear in my mind. Climbing down the hill from the road, the church people gathered there, and my sister playing the accordion. My dress was lavender with a purple band around the bottom of the skirt about three inches above the hem. With my head down, I stared at that purple stripe. I felt like I was being marched to my death.

As they sang "Shall We Gather at the River", I was led into the murky waters. I have no idea what the pastor said before he placed his hand on my forehead and pushed me backwards into the water. I was terrified.

I lived. And it was another ritual I had endured to please my mother, my church and my God.

A marriage, three children and twelve moves later, we began attending a church by Lake Overholser near Oklahoma City. One Sunday the pastor talked about being baptized. His description of baptism did not in any way match my experience. As I listened to him talk, I was fascinated to learn that this was a symbolic way to show the death of our old nature and a sign of our new birth in Christ. This action signified to others that we believed in Christ's death and resurrection. Even more than that was the idea that being baptized told others we had a new identification. We belonged to Christ.

I wanted to be baptized. But first I asked if it meant walking out into the lake. I still couldn't swim.

It was a choice I made that day, to step down into the safe, warm waters of the baptistery. My children watched as I emerged from the waters, grinning from ear to ear. I knew what I was doing, and I meant it from the bottom of my heart. I wanted others to know that I had identified with Christ.

Polly

Her name was Polly. She became my Sunday School teacher when I turned ten. The first time I walked into her classroom, she hugged me. I stiffened. My mother never touched me, let alone hugged me. I had no idea how to react.

Polly oozed warmth and caring. She gave us special little presents like a pencil with our own name on it. My name. At home I was invisible. No one called me by name. But here was proof I had one.

I looked forward to Sunday School class; not for the lesson, but for the presence of Polly. I felt loved in that room.

When I transitioned on to the next class and teacher, Polly kept in touch with me. She would find me at church and give me one of those hugs that became so very important to me. She still gave me little gifts. She continued to make me feel special, at least for the moments I was around her. I didn't know how to tell her thank you. Words would not have been enough. I couldn't verbalize what she had done for me on the inside.

Polly has been gone for many years. But I know one of the "stars" in her crown is because of the love she showed in that little girl's Sunday School class. We learned so much more than words on a page.

For me, she was Jesus with skin on.

Notches in Your Belt

I became acquainted with April when I got a new job. We were both single. What an unlikely pair we were. I came from a strict religious background that had a list of sins. April had no "thou shalt nots". She lived with Gene, an arrangement that was in its fourth year when I met her.

We shared stories. She had married at the age of 16, had two little girls and widowed by the age of 19. I had married at 17, had three girls and then my husband left.

Many of our talks centered around my beliefs as a Christian. As we explored together, I came to the realization that my list of rules did not constitute being a Christian. April wanted to know more about this "Jesus" guy. She purchased a Bible and sent Gene packing. I began to understand that judging others was not my mission in life. Our growth continued.

My church announced a women's retreat. It took me days to decide that maybe April would like to go with me. We talked it over. After many questions, she agreed to go.

Free time on Saturday and April wanted some time to stroll around the campground. Several women gathered around the fireplace in the lodge and I joined them. The talk turned to evangelism. One lady in particular, Gloria, was being very vocal about what she thought. Finally I could contain myself no longer. I quietly talked of caring about the other person, getting to know them and where they were coming from. Gloria returned even stronger. Our duty was to bring them to the Lord by knocking on their door or cornering them on the street. I requested that April be allowed to just get used to being around a group of Christians, to allow her trust to grow.

Sunday morning was the final service. Once again, April wanted to sit near the back. It was a pleasant time and drawing to a close with an altar call. Oh no! Heads were bowed. Suddenly Gloria appeared at our row and pushed her way past several ladies to stand beside April.

Not at all quietly, she told April it was time for her to come to the front of the chapel and accept Christ. April whispered "no". Gloria loudly urged her, this time taking her hand and pulling on her arm. April whispered "no".

I wanted to stick my fist in the Gloria's face.

Finally, April gave in to the pulling and allowed herself to be led to the front. I followed along behind, not knowing what to do. Loudly Gloria prayed and told April what to say. My thoughts were such a jumble. Why had Gloria done this?

Gloria decided April was through and stood to smile at everyone. April and I quietly walked to the back of the chapel, and April kept on walking. I grabbed our purses and left too.

April was very quiet. Too quiet. What could I say?

"April, I'm so sorry. I had no idea someone would do that". Still silent, she pulled out her suitcase and began to pack. I copied her actions. She rolled up her sleeping bag. So did I. Soon we were in her car, bouncing down the gravel road. As we drove onto the highway and picked up speed, her torrent started. She became a little, dark volcano spewing everywhere.

"Why? Why? Why did she do that? Did that make her feel like a big shot? I told her no. Why did she keep pulling? I went with her just to get her to shut up. Does she have ears? I SAID NO."

The miles and the words kept flying by. "I felt like a notch in her belt".

Sounded like a good analogy to me.

The trip took three hours and she was still spewing when we got home.

As April let me out at my house, she said, "Don't ever ask me to go to church with you again." And she drove off. Gloria had destroyed so much.

The next Sunday, from my place on the front row of the choir, I looked directly into the smiling face of Gloria sitting in the front row of the congregation. The pastor talked excitedly of the reports from the retreat and of a major victory in leading an unchurched person to Christ. I felt like throwing up, as Gloria smiled and nodded.

Evangelism is not about "notches in your belt".

Does Your Wife Have a Name?

The church we attended had a new pastor, John Calhoun. So, my husband, Ray, invited him over for dinner. John's wife would not be coming with him, because she was a teacher and would be finishing up her school year in another state. This information amazed me. He was letting his wife stay? I wasn't allowed out of our house without Ray.

When John arrived, Ray escorted him to the patio where they dined on steak and salad. I had hamburgers in the house with the children. This was not an unusual arrangement for me. That's just how it was.

Apparently, John did not understand the situation. He came in the house and began to try to have a conversation with me. It was a strange game we played. John would ask me a question and Ray would answer. I knew my job was to stay out of the way for the evening.

Finally, John asked Ray, "Does your wife have a name?"

I felt the impact of that question in the pit of my stomach. Why did this man want to know my name? I was never called by name. After John left, I received the expected lecture about what my place was in our marriage. I hoped that would be the end of it.

John's wife, Jan, arrived in town. She was very friendly to me at church, always with a big smile on her face. I could barely make eye contact.

One Saturday Ray answered the doorbell and there stood Jan. She said, "I've come to take Lois shopping." This was news to me. But Ray explained that I didn't go shopping. He bought whatever I needed and brought it home to me. Jan would not drop it. She kept pushing. I began to get nervous. Ray would not like this. I was astonished when he finally agreed to let me go. But Jan pushed some more.

"She will need some money if she's going shopping."

I was never allowed to have money. But to my amazement, Ray took out $20 and began to hand it to Jan. She laughed and said, "Oh, that's not nearly enough and besides you need to hand it to Lois." This was getting a bit too much for me. My mind leapt ahead to what my consequence would be.

My mouth fell open when Ray handed ME $50!

I was like a child at Disneyland for the first time. I didn't know how to say what I was looking for, because I didn't know the choices. I stuttered and stumbled my way through conversation with Jan. This was all new territory.

I bought a dress, a blue sheath with white polka dots. Since Ray's mother's favorite color was red, most of my clothes were that color. I didn't care for red. Jan delivered me to my door with my treasure. My purchase was not discussed. Maybe I had made it through unscathed.

Sunday morning, I put on my new dress. Was it ok to think I looked nice in it? Or would God get me for thinking that? Again, no mention of the new purchase as we climbed in the car for church.

John stood at the door, greeting his congregation as they arrived. When it was my turn, he shook my hand and told me how very nice I looked in my new dress. I lowered my head and hurried by. I knew Ray had heard him.

Within a few months, we moved to a different state. The reason I was given for the sudden move was that Ray could see that I was having an affair with John. He needed to get me away from him.

My life did not change abruptly because of the interaction with John and Jan. But a seed had been planted, a seed that said I had some worth as a person. This story took place in 1970, but I can still remember every detail of the beginning of hope that blossomed under the encouragement of two believers who understood more than I thought they did.

The Peanut Butter Jar

Having been raised to believe God was waiting around the next corner to "zap" me if I breathed wrong, I was filled with fear and hopelessness. At the age of 15, my mother allowed the church to begin making arrangements for my marriage to the preacher's son. Totally aware I had no choice in the matter I accepted that fate and married when I was barely 17, leaving high school and moving to another state. Mental and emotional abuses were added to my already oppressed life. And then, after 13 years, he left.

Battered, bruised, no self-confidence and feeling hopeless, it took me two years to get the courage to decide I even had any value worth working on. As my confidence slowly grew, I joined a church choir.

Then came the weekend that the choir went away for a retreat.

I was terrified but longed to be included. I had no extra money, but someone offered to pay my way. Someone else gave me a ride in their car. That's how I ended up sitting at the feet of a man named Bob Benson. His words helped change my life.

He was a scrawny, little man with a timid sounding voice. He had no grand gestures or extreme passion. But he was so very real. I drank in his words. He began to speak of having crystal glasses and china dishes in the cupboard. I couldn't relate. We had never had either. He talked of how those glasses and dishes were saved for "good", .and how wasted they were, because "good" only happened once or twice a year.

His words turned to the peanut butter jar. It comes home in the grocery bag. Someone puts it in the cupboard. The kids get it out to make sandwiches. Over the days, it becomes empty. Somehow it ends up in the dishwasher. When the clean dishes are taken out of the dishwasher, the empty peanut butter jar is placed in the cupboard with part of the label still stuck on. Someone is thirsty, reaches in the cupboard and gets the jar to use for a drink. And the cycle begins. It goes back in the dishwasher. Maybe this time it gets chipped or a little bit more of the label comes off. But it is a vital part of the daily life.

While that picture was clear in our minds, he opened his Bible to Colossians 1:27b.

"For this is the secret, Christ lives in you."

He began to explain how we are all vessels. Some are like the exquisite crystal and they rarely do "good". I'm sure my eyes opened wider and wider. These were the people I had been taught to revere and model after. Somehow, I was just never was quite "good" enough.

When he began to talk about the "peanut butter jar" people, tears ran down my cheeks. There I sat, with my jar chipped and labeled. But he was telling me I was a vessel; one that could be a vital part of the everyday life of the Christian.

I didn't change overnight. It was a slow process. But I had a secret. Christ was in ME. My job was to be the vessel. I sat a peanut butter jar on our counter at home as a constant reminder. I knew with every fiber of my being that I could be a peanut butter jar!

I have turned to that scripture again and again. The Message Bible says, "The mystery in a nutshell is just this: Christ is in you. It's that simple."

The vessel is not the important part. It is what we contain.

You may not be a "peanut butter jar", but I'm sure you know someone who is. They may be very quiet and distant, or rough around the edges with tattoos and piercings. Perhaps they are just angry. Maybe, like I was, they have a lot of illnesses that are psychosomatic. They just don't know it yet, but they can be vessels containing a secret, Christ. It is our job to let them in on that secret.

Each time I see a peanut butter jar, I am reminded of that evening long ago. Bob Benson didn't have a pulpit made out of wood. He stood in front of a fireplace. But that night he became my minister as he opened the scriptures for me.

I may be chipped and still have some label stuck on me, but I am a vessel containing the incredible secret that Christ lives in me.

Gift or Burden

When I began dating my husband, John, I started attending his church. He really wanted me to get acquainted with Molly, the lady who was church secretary and lady's Bible study leader. I tried. Yet each time I came in contact with her, I was so very uncomfortable. Being around her was not something I wanted to do. When John asked "why?" I had no answer. I just knew I had very strong feelings about it.

Our relationship grew serious and marriage was discussed. John assumed the pastor of his church, Peter, would perform the ceremony. I was very uncomfortable with that idea. When John asked "why?" I had no answer. And so, an Associate Pastor officiated at our wedding.

A few months later, an Elder announced from the pulpit that Peter was no longer the pastor. As happens in all groups of people, the reason he was gone soon filtered down. Peter had been having an affair with Molly.

Now I understood my reluctance to be around them.

The church began auditioning for a new pastor. One Sunday, when one of the candidates began preaching, I got up and walked out of church. I don't do things like that. But the "vibes" coming from him were so strong I could not stay in the building.

Again, John wanted to know "why?" and I had no answer. I remember saying, "I sure hope they don't hire him".

They did.

I struggled to attend church. I could not hear the words coming from his mouth because I was so uncomfortable being in the same room with him. My attention and energy were focused on making it through to the end of the service. Everything within me wanted to walk out again.

In a matter of months, he was no longer pastor. It had been discovered that he beat his wife. Now I understood why I had such a reaction to being around him.

I never know when I will begin to feel something. I can go for weeks without it happening. And I don't always find out the reason for my reaction. But I've learned to be very aware of the "vibes" I receive from people.

The gift of discernment is not an easy gift to accept. I didn't ask for this gift. In fact, I fought against the idea that I did indeed have it. Sometimes, being in a crowd of people is totally overwhelming. There can be waves of what I call "vibes" bombarding me.

I have been told I am judgmental, weird and scary. Sometimes I am sure I come across as arrogant, although I try to be kind. But when I get the feeling that something is not right, I am very sure about it. A few times, the feeling has been so strong that the very hairs on the back of my neck have stood straight up. It's hard to smile and be nice when your very being is poised to run from the encounter.

Having this gift requires me to be extra cautious about voicing my reaction. John has learned to live with it, but others are uncomfortable when I share with them about my "gift".

I Cor. 12:11 says, "It is the one and only Holy Spirit who distributes these gifts. He alone decides which gift each person should have." This is a special ability I believe God has given me. It is my desire to use it wisely.

Extended Family

What an eclectic group of people. And they arrive at our house every Wednesday evening as part of what our church calls a "Care Group".

Betty and Norma are the octogenarians of the bunch. Both single ladies, they are full of vim and vigor. Yet they both have reasons to be "stay-at-home" senior citizens. Norma's heart does not work well. She has been known to sneak a pill during our meeting because of the angina pain. Her arthritis has caused enlargement of her joints and constant pain. Her love for the Lord shines through it all.

A few years ago, Betty wasn't feeling well. She put off saying anything until it became an emergency room trip and admission to the hospital. She was prepped for surgery, but the bile had already leaked from the duct and when they opened her up, her abdomen was contaminated.

Her coma lasted for days. The doctors and nurses advised her daughter, Connie, to "pull the plug". Connie's response was "You don't know my mother". The family gathered. Our group took food, prayers and hugs to them.

Betty survived. She is now as active as she ever was.

Roy is retired. But he is busier than ever. As head of the local Christian Motorcycle Association, he travels a lot, sometimes from one coast to the other, always sharing Christ at rest areas and restaurants. Once a year he goes with a group of men to take motorcycles to South America and deliver them to the pastors who have to travel many miles to visit outlying villages.

Bruce and Betty used to be regular attendees. Then Hurricane Katrina arrived. They loaded up their RV and headed to the devastation. As a retired insurance adjuster, Bruce was hired back to help with the overload. Even though they have a beautiful four-bedroom home here, they have continued to live in their RV and have now moved their efforts to Florida. Sometimes they have as many as 40 people eating the wonderful food Betty loves to cook. We still consider them one of us.

One member of our group, Sharon, a single lady whose profession is nursing, lost her job and we helped her through those months of depression and fear until she could get on her feet again.

Rich is a high school teacher who rides the 30 miles back and forth to work on a motorcycle. He and his wife, Jennie, live on the edge of town and have various animals from horses to goats and chickens. We've helped them pray through the issues of being landlords, changing jobs and children growing up. Recently, we got to celebrate the birth of their first grandchild.

Lori is a single lady who moved here from the L.A. area, because she wanted to live some place that was safer. As a baby Christian, we got the pleasure of watching her blossom into a "Christ Follower" that eagerly shares her love for the Lord with others. As she now works full time and is attending college, she has moved to a group that meets on Sunday evenings.

Martin and Naomi used to be a part of our group. They had already adopted one daughter from China, who they named Carol. Then they chose to do it again, only this time for a "special needs" child. When they came home with "Hope", we moved our gathering to their house to give Hope time to adapt in her own new environment. Recently, they decided to move their time for gathering to Sunday night, which worked better with their schedule.

Mary and Jack joined us a few years ago. He was the quiet, steady one and she was full of energy and questions. She delighted in making flower arrangements for weddings and was developing a thriving home-based business. Then came the day in August 2005, that she and their daughter were murdered in their own home.

Our little group was in shock. But we gathered around Jack and his family. Due to the circumstances, the funerals had to be postponed until the bodies were released. That meant a long time of waiting for the family. We took food and warm bodies to sit and grieve with them. And then, three days after the tragedy, Jack gave back to me. Sitting on the patio, talking quietly, he said the words that I will never forget. "I have Jesus".

That's what a "care group" is all about. Taking care of each other and "having Jesus".

Worldwide Access

For several years, my husband, John, and I regularly traveled to Sandpoint, Idaho; restoring our hearts, souls and minds on the shores of Lake Pend Oreille. Of course, sitting on the deck at Starbucks was one of the requirements to achieve restoration.

One summer day, the conversation at the table next to us caught our attention. Apparently, those two young men had started a new church in the area. They were discussing the pros and cons of having "care groups". Since we are the shy, retiring types, we broke into their conversation to share the pros we have experienced in our own care group. During the conversation, the name of their new church was mentioned… Cedar Hills.

Time passed and some summers went by. John and I decided to go to Sandpoint over the 4th of July weekend. That meant we would be there on a Sunday. On Saturday evening, almost simultaneously, we began to talk of visiting the church we had previously heard about. I pulled the name "Cedar Hills" from the recesses of my mind. John wondered if his shorts and sandals attire would be appropriate to wear.

Sunday morning, we asked the young lady at the front desk of our motel if she had heard of it. She was delighted to give us directions, as she had attended there. It was a warehouse. Before we entered the "sanctuary", an older lady behind a welcome desk offered each of us a packet containing earplugs. Just how loud was the music?

It was loud, but we kept the plugs in our pockets. Coffee urns were along the side. Folding chairs made up the pews. As we looked around, we could see the average age of the attendees was probably 35. They regularly re-filled their coffee cups during the service. The preacher had on shorts and sandals. He referred to their church as "the gathering". But I clearly remember his message.

A few years later, to celebrate John's 60th birthday, we arranged a family gathering over the 4th of July weekend in Bend, Oregon. When John and I arrived in town, we stopped to get a bite to eat. As we were being seated in the restaurant, we passed a booth where a young man sat reading the Bible. John said, "good book", as we walked by.

After placing our orders, John returned to the booth to talk with the man. He was a pastor, working on his Sunday sermon. His church had no building but met on the grounds of an elementary school in the area. When John returned to our booth, he was equipped with a map showing us the way for Sunday.

John and I, our children and grandchildren sat on folding chairs on the lawn, in the bright morning sunshine, with the sounds in the background of children enjoying the playground. Once again, the pastor had on shorts and sandals. And once again, I remembered his message. In the days and weeks afterward, one of our daughters referred to that specific sermon as a guiding light in helping her with a major decision.

We are members of a local congregation. We have a beautiful new "worship center". John and I attend regularly and serve in various roles within the church. I remember many of the sermons from the lips of our pastor. I feel blessed to be a part of this congregation.

But that is not the "church". No matter where I might travel in the world, if I seek it, I can find the "church". It might be in someone's home or in an unused movie theater. The building is not the important part. The people who gather to meet with the Lord are the "church" and you can meet them in airports and subways, on busy streets or on a farm.

I may be far from home, but in visiting with the stranger next to me, it doesn't take long to discover whether they are a member of the same "church" as me; that we are following the same "Christ". This allows us to speak the same language.

I've prayed with strangers, sometimes before I even know their name. I've given a good Christian book to someone who hasn't read it and received books in the same manner. When your soul connects with another Christian, you are suddenly friends.

Christians have worldwide access to other Christians, known as the "church".

Expectations

We all have them. By definition, expectations are just that, something expected. It is not written in stone that expectations will be fulfilled or indeed that one has any right they should be.

I found a list of relationship expectations.

- That the right man/woman will fix my life
- For women – that he will call all the shots and make all the money
- For men – that she will naturally be better at domestic chores
- For men – that she will also be less capable at everything else
- That if it's true love, he/she will know what I want without me having to ask
- That the relationship will always remain the same

All of these expectations are unrealistic!

The media is full right now of talk about shows dealing with body makeovers. The contestants have HUGE expectations that are unrealistic and unhealthy about what the results will be. Of concern is the young impressionable audience watching these shows who are already self-conscious about their body image. If they buy into these expectations, they may be setting themselves up for a lifetime of unmet expectations and failure.

Your idea of what a "good mother" should be has likely been built up to such an unrealistic level by magazine articles and advice books that you may exhaust yourself trying. That may leave you with little tolerance for the many minor problems that naturally arise. What happens to the joy of being a parent?

What about Christians? What can we expect from God's people? We all have a set of expectations for our church. Many of us simply expect that the church will always be like Jesus. Are those expectations reasonable, much less Biblical? My church did a study in the book of Acts for 40 days. Acts is full of conflict, complaints, dissension, factions and unmet expectations.

I learned years ago, that a church is full of people who are going to act like people. They may disappoint us, hurt us and tick us off. No church will mesh perfectly with our ideal of what the church is supposed to be. The ideal church is only in our head.

There is only one Person who can meet ALL expectations. So, we might as well learn how to get along in the only church we have here on earth.

Clearly, all expectations cannot be met. What happens then?

Reactions to unmet expectations run the gamut from disappointment to murder. Unmet expectations may lead to an unhealthy anger. We are the only ones who can deal with our own unmet expectations.

Perhaps we may need to permanently let go of them. We may feel a sense of loss at giving up an ideal we have held for many years. Sometimes we can find an alternative to meet our expectations. When I first wanted to lose weight, I needed to lose 100 pounds. It would have been very unrealistic of me to expect to lose that much weight in three months. When I altered my expectations to lose it over the period of two years, I was able to meet my expectations.

Expectations usually come from a deep yearning we have. You may need acceptance. Your expectation is that you receive that acceptance from one specific person. However, you may need to realize that you can receive acceptance from someone else.

Due to my mother's unrealistic expectations of me, I had no childhood. Due to my expectations of what "mother" meant, I never felt accepted by her. In my first marriage, my efforts to attain my husband's unrealistic expectations of me damaged my health to the point of hospitalization. I became unhealthy because I was striving for acceptance by him. It took me several years to analyze and reject unwanted expectations for me and for others by me.

I urge you to take a look at your expectations. Are they causing a problem in your life? Now is the time to deal with them, before your unrealistic expectations lead you to years of illnesses, dysfunction or even death. Expending your energy on unrealistic expectations only leads to disappointment and imbalance in your life.

My life would have been so very different if I had only understood the ramifications for my future due to the expectations placed on me from others. That understanding would have allowed me to focus my energy on my own personal growth; thereby enabling me to become an encouragement to others.

How realistic are your expectations?

The Real Thing

I am a NASCAR fan. Whenever possible, I watch the whole race. I'm familiar with the tracks, the announcers, the drivers and their families and the sponsors. I know the rules and am immediately aware if a driver breaks one. I make occasional comments and noises as the race unfolds. My husband tells me he enjoys watching me watch the race.

Sometimes I have to record the race and watch it later. I've learned to NEVER talk to anyone who has already seen the end of the race. I say, "Please don't tell me anything, because I haven't seen it yet" and then they say something like, "Ok, but he sure is cute." How many cute drivers do you think there are? One time the comment was, "Ok, but the winner broke a record". I instantly knew the winner was Dale Jarrett. I was aware that if he won, he would break a record.

One August my family reunion was held at my older brother's house in Colorado. That weekend was the inaugural "Brickyard" race. Some of the reunion was held in the yard and others of us were in the living room, yelling for our favorites.

Then I actually attended a race. Believe me, there is no comparison between watching it on television and actually being there. The sounds, smells and noises almost overwhelm your senses.

Watching it on television would never be the same again. I knew more than I used to. I was aware of so many "behind the scenes" activities that you never see on the screen. And when the race is at the track where I actually sat in the stands, it's like old home week. A piece of me is still there. There is no way I can convey to another person exactly what it was like to be there. Their attendance at a race is the only way they can know for themselves.

I find a lot of parallels between my illustration about following the NASCAR circuit and about following Christ.

I am a Christian. I began attending church when I was a week old. We went twice on Sunday and once in the middle of the week. When there was a revival, we were there every night. I was familiar with the scriptures, knew how to pray, was acquainted with the other members of the congregation and knew exactly what God expected of me. I had the list of rules.

I was not alone in my beliefs. I was surrounded by people with the same ones. And so, I did not understand there was anything better.

Flat on my back in a hospital bed, with a specialist looking down at me explaining what my medical issues were, for the first time, I talked to God. That is how the relationship began, having conversations with the maker of the universe … and me.

Over the ensuing weeks, I began to understand the scripture that says to "pray continuously". It became another form of breathing for me, as I grew in my faith and my health improved. As the months passed, I became aware of a deep abiding peace in my soul. Years of attending church had never given that to me. I desired to pray. Knowing how to pray for so many years had never given me the desire for more time with God.

There is no comparison between going to church, doing all the right things, avoiding the wrong things and actually having a relationship with God. Sometimes the feelings of relief, of being safe, of being loved and cared for are overwhelming. I stand in awe of a "Presence" within and around me.

Attending church is not the same. I no longer go because "they" expect it, or for others to see how "good" I am. I go because it is a priority to me. I see the others who are going through the motions and I understand that they have never yet had the relationship. And until they personally have that communion with God, they will never understand my puny efforts to explain it to them.

But having tasted the "real thing", it is hard to be patient. I want to shake them by the shoulders and say, "You don't know what you're missing".

You can hear my passion and excitement about racing in my voice when I talk about it. I pray that when I talk about my relationship with God, I convey the same passion and excitement.

Cart Before the Horse

Write a book! She had to be joking! I stared at my friend/employer, Meri-lyn, and then burst out laughing. She was an English professor, of course she wasn't serious. But she continued talking. "Joy, do you have any idea how many students I use you as an example for? You really should write a book."

She was serious.

I pondered her words. My growth in becoming a whole person was evident to family and friends alike. Anyone who had known me "before" said there was no resemblance to the "after". I had become a totally different person inside and out. But I hadn't realized I was being used as an example; that unknown others would care about what was happening in my life.

In my growth, I had learned to weigh all possibilities offered. No longer did I automatically reject a goal which I thought far beyond my reach. I had already attained too many "unreachable" ones.

And so, I prayed, "Lord, if this is guidance from you, I need some affirma-tion". I let it rest and had almost forgotten it.

A few weeks later, I found myself in my pastor's office, seeking advice on how to handle a new complication in my life. When that discussion seemed to be concluded, he reached in his desk and took out a three-ring binder. Handing it to me, he said, "Joy, you need to start writing down what you are experiencing. Some day you are going to write a book."

I had asked for affirmation yet hadn't really expected any. Suddenly, I realized this was no joke. Two people, within a few weeks time, had urged me to share what was happening in my life to help others. And I did, sincerely, want to help others who were hurting.

About the same time, I became acquainted with a pastor of a different church, who was struggling with starting a singles group. Since I was single, he began to pick my brain about what it was like.

Then came the day he asked me to go away for the weekend with his singles group and be the speaker. The pact I had made with my "new" self was to say "yes" instead of "no" because of fear. So, I agreed to do it.

I began to feel important. Others needed me. I had words to say that others wanted to hear. I got sidetracked helping others (which I truly did want to do) but getting the "big head" because I had experienced so much and could be of such invaluable service. I had never felt needed before in my life and I certainly did not do a very good job of handling it.

In essence, I was given a good "slap on my hand" and put on hold. Suddenly my writing was stilted and that weekend away, I truly messed up. I had a burning desire to write and speak, but I had moved into high gear without allowing any preparation time. The brakes slammed on so hard I could smell the rubber burning.

Yes, I had accomplished a lot. I had overcome a great deal of bad programming. I had lost 100 pounds. I had made a new life for me and my children. And I realized that that is exactly how I saw it. "I" had done it.

So, I worked on me some more. For the first 30 years of my life I had not been given credit for anything. I wanted so badly to say, "see what I have done". But as I read my Bible and prayed, meditated and waited on God, I received a much clearer picture of what had really transpired.

God had done it. I was just the broken vessel that He mended.

This new understanding didn't happen overnight. It took me years to catch on how to be in the background again. I fought it. I had earned my place, me and me alone.

Funny thing, that's not how God saw it.

And so, once again, I'm trying my writing and speaking wings. But this time, I am very aware of where my strength comes from, the source of my ideas and the passion I feel for those hurting. I've been given a gift to use to help others. It is up to me to put the words on paper or into the air. I am only the channel used to transmit information.

The rest is up to God.

The Proposition

He was looking directly at me.

"Is there somewhere we can go to meet discreetly? I think we could enjoy our bodies together."

I looked around the foyer of the church. Was this man talking to me? Had anyone heard his question? A myriad of thoughts flew through my head. He was suggesting such things here, in church! The two couldn't seem to go together. He was a professor of religion at the college where I worked. I knew his wife.

I had been a non-person, functioning in an arranged marriage and then my husband left me. In my journey of starting over, I moved to a different state and took a job at a church college. This allowed me to talk with many professors. We would discuss a wide range of topics; from raising kids to spiritual matters. I was in the process of learning to choose my own opinion instead of what my mother, my church, and my husband had decided was right. So I enjoyed these discussions immensely. It gave me opportunity to explore new concepts.

Several times this particular professor and I had talked; nice friendly talks, interesting and thought provoking. He had spoken of the changes in me. I was developing a personality, improving my health and appearance by diet and exercise and learning how to dress in contemporary styles.

For the first time in my life I was beginning to feel good about myself as a woman. He assumed from the talk of my history (and rightly so) that anything sexual had certainly been merely a wifely duty to be performed and I had never known pleasure.

Now he was offering to teach me what I needed to know. An attractive professor; not some bum, was propositioning me. And such questions. I was so shocked, I don't remember my responses, but they contained a large NO.

But he wouldn't take no for an answer. He called me at work. I would run into him walking across the campus with students passing by. They would never believe the conversation taking place here. I repeated my no answer on a regular basis. Even though I never really had a battle saying no to him, I desired to experience what he talked about.

My life went on. I kept growing and becoming. Part of that process involved changing jobs, going to work in a nearby town. One day I ran into him in the grocery store. I was relieved to tell him I would be working in another town and probably wouldn't see him again.

"Great. That will make it all the easier to meet discreetly. Shall we try it?"

It would have been a tantalizing excursion into the forbidden. Who knows what the consequences would have been. It could have destroyed his family and caused a break in my relationship with my own children. And what would have happened to the new found feelings I had of myself, that I was a person of value?

With God's help, I didn't go there. My answer remained a steadfast no.

Starbucks Gang

The church I grew up in had a lot of rules. One of their basic tenets was "come ye out from among them and be ye separate". That meant, "Do not have anything to do with anyone who does not go to this church". Therefore, I could not attend school functions or play with the neighbor children. They were going to hell.

Little did I realize that my reputation was totally tied to my attendance at that church. Years later, at a high school reunion, I discovered that the people who went there were viewed as arrogant and elitist, including me.

During the years of my first marriage, my duty was to be in my house cleaning, cooking and taking care of the children. No friends were allowed. Only after my first husband left me, did I come to understand that my neighbors thought I had mental issues because I wasn't social. They didn't realize they were going to hell and I had to stay away so I wouldn't be dragged there with them.

Then came my years of discovery and liberation. Such a relief and sense of freedom.

And so began my pursuit of social skills. There were people everywhere. If you talked to them, most of them would respond. And they weren't evil.

I now attend a wonderful church. There is a core group of people who arrive every Sunday. But our goal is to see new faces, more and more of them, each time our doors are open. We don't want them to stay away. Hopefully, we have a reputation as a warm and welcoming church. I have made good friends there.

I know my neighbors. Their children talk to me over the fence as I work in the yard. I love it. More friends.

At work I interact with people I know are not Christians. I'm there for a reason. So they can see Christ. I can't show them that by shutting them out. More friends.

The places of business I enter on a regular basis, such as my bank, employ people who I call by their first name (including the President). They may or may not be a Christian, but that cannot be an issue in whether I reach out to them. They've become my friends. For my 65th birthday, I received a card signed by all of them.

When my husband, John, and I first started going to Starbucks, we would stand in line and see the group gathered in the corner, laughing and talking. John and I sat at a table, carrying on our conversation, wondering what that group represented.

Then one day, we were sitting close enough to hear the conversation. One of the questions was directed to us. That is how it began. We became a part of that group in the corner, laughing and talking. Slowly, we learned their names, their occupations and what they loved in life, mostly motorcycles and cars.

This past Thanksgiving, we were invited to one of their cabins in the mountains to spend the day with their family, eating and laughing and playing in the snow. When we had a problem with a trio of skunks making a home under our deck, one of the "gang" brought over his traps and carried them off one at a time.

We celebrate each other's birthdays and we care when one of the "gang" has a medical problem. It's like an extended family. This group is a mix of people who have gravitated together over a period of time.

It's delightful to drive to Starbucks on a Saturday morning, buy our drinks, and then join the "Starbucks Gang" for a time of discussion about anything and almost everything. The guy who works for the city can tell us what is being built across the street. The lady who works for the telephone company can give us an answer to a question about phone lines. Some of them pour concrete and some of them come dressed in suits and ties and are lawyers.

Since I moved from oppression to freedom, I've discovered many things. I've learned there are good people everywhere. People who love life and care about the kinds of things I care about. Yes, I've met a few of the bad ones, and I've been taken advantage of. But that does not distort my outlook on life. Not when I can have a delicious flavored steamer (I don't like coffee) as I visit with the 'Starbucks Gang".

No Do-Overs

I knew how to be a parent. There were many role models in my large family, and of course my church gave me more families to observe. The goal was to be in control of your children. If the stern look and the snapping of the fingers didn't work, then sometimes a spanking or a good washing of the mouth with soap would help.

That's the way I was raised.

Marriage at 17 and my first child at 19. No problem. And then two more children in quick succession. I could handle this. If I didn't, I would get the flak for their misbehaviors. Since their father was the preacher, they were required to sit unmoving and quiet in the front of the church. It was my job to make sure that happened.

I had been trained to never let any softness show. That would mean you were weak. No hugging, no touching and certainly no telling them "I love you". That would make you vulnerable.

I had it down to a science.

Then my husband left me. Suddenly, I was going to have to go to work. What would happen to the children's discipline? Who would be there to make them toe the mark?

The next few years were a struggle in many ways; financially, emotionally and physically. I searched for understanding about myself. Why did I operate the way I did? Did I like it? What could I do about it?

I discovered I didn't like me at all. I wanted to be a different kind of parent, one who hugged their children and told them they were loved. I gathered them in the living room and explained, "I don't like the way I've been a mom to you. From now on, I am going to hug you and kiss you and tell you I love you." They had no idea how to react to that.

And I began to analyze my answers to them. Why had I said that? What did I really think? One day my 12-year old daughter asked if she could get her ears pierced. I let loose with my answer.

"I can't believe you would want to do such a thing. Only sluts have their ears pierced. You know we don't believe in that. Now go in your room and never ask me that again."

Matter solved. Over and done with.

But I could hear my answer playing back in my head. Those were my Mother's words. What did I really think about pierced ears? I had no idea.

I knocked softly on my daughter's bedroom door. Poking my head in, I said, "You know what? I don't really know what I think about you getting your ears pierced. Give me a week to think about it and I'll let you know".

In the grand scheme of things, with all the issues involved in raising teenagers, what was the problem with pierced ears? I couldn't come up with a real good reason to say "no".

A week later, I put my arm around my daughter and said, "Let's go get our ears pierced".

I know I inflicted emotional damage on my children when they were young. I did it because it was all I knew. And I could spend the rest of my life feeling guilty about my role in causing some of the issues they have had to deal with. But I cannot go back and re-do their childhood. It is what it is.

Just as I have had to work through the way I was raised, they have to sort through their own baggage. I cannot do it for them.

I have gone to each one of them and asked for forgiveness. I told them I was available to talk with about their childhood issues, and I would answer them honestly. We have had some great heart-to-hearts. On the other hand, one of them disowned me and had no contact for 12 years.

Does that hurt? Badly. Yet I cannot fix it. My job is to pray and love.

I know God wants them to lead "abundant" lives. If I am part of the plan for them to reach that, then I am ready to help. The results are in God's hands.

Groceries and Hats

My days were filled with taking care of the house and children, and still trying to be a perfect preacher's wife. That was my identity. One day my husband, Ray, came home talking excitedly. There was a new concept in health care, called Medi-Centers. He had read about them in a magazine.

I failed to understand why Ray even cared about this, let alone be so animated. He informed me he was going to write and see if they had any new ones being built. He was leaving the ministry. He wanted to become an administrator of one.

He was giving up preaching! It was up to me to deal with it, no questions asked.

Events occurred rapidly and soon Ray was being flown to Memphis for training. I was left at home to pack. Groceries were purchased before he left, and I was told to "make do" until he returned in two weeks.

I ran out of food and had no idea how to get more. My neighbor, Peggy, worked in a bank. Even though I had been told to have no contact with her (she was divorced) I was desperate.

I called her. "Peggy, this is very embarrassing for me, but Ray didn't leave me with enough groceries to last until he comes back. Could I possibly borrow enough money to at least buy some hamburger and milk?"

I was shocked when her answer was an immediate "No". It had been so very hard to ask. Now what would I do?

"Do you have a joint checking account?"

"I don't know."

"Just a minute and I'll check". Silence on the other end of the phone. I wasn't sure what she was talking about.

"Yes, you do have a joint checking account. That means you have access to your own money".

"But Ray told me he had used it all to buy me the groceries before he left".

"Do you know how to check on your balance?"

"No."

"Do you know your account number?"

"No."

"Write these numbers down" and she proceeded to give me my account number. "Now I am going to transfer you to someone else. Tell them your account number and ask them what the balance is in that account."

As I puzzled over what she had said, another voice came on asking if they could help me. I followed Peggy's instructions. The voice told me there were several hundred dollars in that account. I said, "Thank you" and hung up.

Now what was I supposed to do? I pondered for quite some time. Then I called the number Ray had left with me in case of emergency. I explained everything I had done. What did he want me to do? Could I use a little of that money to buy some groceries?

After telling me off for involving Peggy, he said I could spend $25 of it, but no more. I thanked him profusely and hung up. I wouldn't have to borrow after all.

The phone rang. It was Peggy. "What did you find out? Do you have any money in your account?"

I told her what I had done, including the phone call to Ray. She was furious with me, ordered me to stay put and she would be right there. I was totally confused. Why had Ray said we had no money, when we did? Why was Peggy leaving her job in the middle of the day to come to my house? And why was she so mad?

Within minutes, she was at my door. She took me by the hand and led me to the couch. She told me I didn't need Ray's approval to spend our money to buy groceries for our children.

My responses seemed to irritate her. She got up and paced as she talked. Soon tears were streaming down her face. Her voice rose and fell as I listened, fascinated by the picture she was painting of a world different from the one I lived in, one where a wife was an equal, had a voice in decisions and made choices too.

She knelt in front of me.

"Let's go buy the groceries you need, and then let's go shopping. Maybe you could spend it all on hats! We'll go in every store."

I could never do that. Maybe Ray needed that money for something else.

Her shoulders fell. I saw such sadness in her eyes, sadness I didn't understand. "O.K.," she said, "let's go to the bank and then go buy your groceries".

Forgiving Mother

I had come a long way on my journey to wholeness. Therefore, I felt ready to help others on their journey. When I had a chance to travel to Vail, Colorado to a single's retreat, it seemed like a great opportunity to watch first-hand how the speakers reached out to the hurting people in attendance.

Our trip took us through Salt Lake City. The group wanted to stop there to go to an amusement park. One of the "rides" at the park required that you all straddle a beam, one person in behind another. I was mortified. My mother would never have allowed such close contact in that position. I refused to go on it.

That reaction would surface again later.

At the retreat, I perused the schedule we received. My eyes caught the title "Inner Healing". That looked like a good one. Since I had achieved my own "inner healing", it would be interesting to see how the leader, "Glaphre Gilliland" got that message across to others.

The session was scheduled for an hour. I took a seat in the back of the room so I could observe not only her, but the participants. Glaphre began by talking about the different kinds of hurts we can have. So far so good. I could do that.

She had us close our eyes. I thought the closing of the eyes was a little hokey, but I did it. She drew us deeper and deeper within ourselves, drawing mental pictures of the ropes that bound us, cutting into our flesh and causing bleeding.

I knew I could never lead a session like this.

Then we were told to create in our minds the image of the person who had hurt us.

"Don't open your eyes. But in your mind, I want you to turn around and see who it is that has you bound".

I knew it wouldn't be my ex or his mother. I had that covered. As I mentally turned around, imagine my surprise to see my mother standing there; holding the ends of some ropes in her hands, ropes that had me bound and bleeding.

This could not be. I had no problem with my mother.

Just as suddenly I recalled the incident in Salt Lake City, where I hadn't joined the others in fun. Why? Because of my mother.

The dam burst and the flood began. Memory after memory of mother, always stern and judgmental, telling me what I was doing wrong. Vivid memories. Painful ones. They just kept coming.

Somehow, I got out of that room and found a spot away from the crowd. I felt beaten and bruised. My mother!

I hadn't arrived at all. I was just beginning again.

Every where I turned, something reminded me of mother and her unyielding position of control and judgment. I was afraid to open my mouth. It might be mother talking.

Recovering from my new insights took many months. Two steps forward and one step back, and then sliding all the way to the bottom to start over. The thought resounded in my head…my mother.

Forgiveness is a strange process. There are many definitions of forgiveness. The one I heard the most was, "Forgive and forget". Yet, how could I just forget the first 30 years of my life?

I envisioned traveling back to Kansas to confront my mother. The more I thought about it the more I knew it just wouldn't work. She was in her 70's. She had no idea she needed forgiveness. I would have to do it another way.

As each memory came sweeping through, I consciously chose to forgive. Some memories returned again and again. I still chose to forgive. Over the weeks and months, I made the choice to forgive repeatedly.

When my sister passed away, I traveled to Kansas to the funeral. I put an extra day in, a day to visit with my mother. We laughed together as we had some ice cream. I even spent the night at the home where she was living. We talked late into the night. For the first time in my life, I had an adult conversation with my mother, one where I felt equal.

I hugged and kissed her when it was time to leave. She had no idea the journey I had taken to be able to do that and mean it.

That was the last time I saw her. When she died, I had no guilt, no regrets. I had forgiven.

Cancer and Trust

Due to some medical issues, I suddenly arrived at one of those "life" intersections. The street signs said "Possible Cancer" and "Trust". Before I moved through that intersection, I fell to my knees, shaking, crying and praying.

Cancer is prevalent in my family. I had sisters with breast cancer and one who had both breast and colon cancer. All the horrible implications of that word flew through my head. Is that what I had? I truly wish my immediate reaction had been to place it in God's hands. But for 15 minutes, it was all about me. I stayed stuck at that intersection. As my mind cleared, I knew I had only one choice: trust.

The words of my favorite scripture, Jeremiah 29:11, came to mind. "For I know the plans I have for you, declares the Lord; plans to give you a hope and a future". Those words told me that God knows what He is doing. I didn't have to like it, but this was my journey for now. I called my doctor. He saw me that day, then called to consult with a Gastroenterologist. My appointment with the specialist was scheduled within hours. Gastroenterologist is a big word. It means, "the doctor who looks for cancer in your colon".

I understood the urgency. They had seen my family history. Various tests were scheduled.

Suddenly, the weather forecast was irrelevant. What I had for dinner no longer mattered. There was nothing on television that had any importance. My life became so focused; on God, on prayer, on scripture, on the circle of people around me. I wanted to plead with God to make everything okay but refrained. This happened to other people. Why not me?

At night John, my husband, and I would lie in bed and hold hands. No words were necessary. We would awake in the middle of the night and reach for each other. When I talked about "what if I had cancer", he would change my wording to say, "No, it's what if we have cancer".

Plans were placed on hold. Dinner with friends canceled. We drew in tight together and with God. We were helpless to change the outcome. We had to trust God's wisdom.

As the word "cancer" was floating around in my house, I did a lot of thinking about my life. I thought about what I would do if I was told I had cancer. What would I change? Then I wondered why I would have to wait until I was told I have cancer.

I have been working on me for years now, feeling God was calling me to reach out to women who have been damaged by life. In my few free moments, I would work on writing a little something or maybe on a speech. But my life schedule was a different meeting every evening Monday through Thursday. That didn't leave much quiet time for God, for meditation, for creating words; words to reach others.

These were good meetings, accomplishing good things. But they really weren't taking me in the direction I felt I had been called. I removed myself from three of them. I couldn't give up choir. That was where I got filled again.

Without knowing the final outcome of my medical tests, I decided to take the road called "Trust". My focus turned to the future, however long it was.

And so, I waited.

I drank awful stuff and then had to drink some more. In the pre-dawn darkness, John and I headed for the hospital. I didn't make it all the way. It's a good thing McDonald's is open 24 hours.

The next few days were a blur. I spoke with family on the phone, but have no recollection of doing so. I slept the days away.

And then, having recovered from that, I had the privilege of drinking more horrible liquid that had the consistency of chalk. It's amazing what the medical world does to a person with a health problem.

After several weeks, the diagnosis was given. Big words were used to describe procedures. Lovely pictures were presented to me, along with explanations of my insides. But the words that became music to my ears were, "I removed four "pre-cancerous" polyps. We caught it in time".

I have no formal plan yet. I just know it is time for me to "do" something more. My desire and passion is to help others along their journey. If God had to use the word "cancer" to get my attention, then it worked.

The Yellow Bowl

When I married the first time, one of our wedding presents was a glass set of nesting mixing bowls. The largest of these bowls was yellow. Just the right size for mixing a double batch of cookies.

As the children came along, my desire was for them to have better memories than I had as a child. So that yellow bowl became one of my ways to make memories with my children during the fleeting time they would be under my roof. I sewed us all matching aprons. When we donned our aprons, we were ready for the fun.

A cookbook of just cookie recipes was purchased. We made all kinds. Some we didn't like so much. Others became our "traditions". Sugar cookies became a favorite. This involved a lot of work. Mixing, rolling out the dough, cutting out various shapes, baking them, letting them cool and then the frosting. Sometimes this was a two-day job.

Christmas time was when we specialized. Snickerdoodles rolled in red and green sugars. Candy cane cookies, where half the dough was red and you twisted two strips to make a candy cane. Then someone was given the fun of placing peppermint in a dish towel and using the hammer to break it up. The broken pieces were dropped on the candy cane as it came hot from the oven. Of course, we made sugar cookies frosted in red and green and covered with sprinkles and sugars. While we created with our hands, the aroma of cookies settled into our memories.

And always there was a mess to clean up afterwards.

The girl's friends seemed to appear at cookie-making time, and we made them feel welcome. We taught them the all-important concept of eating cookie dough. A portion of the dough would be set aside, placed in a baggie and stored in the refrigerator. For the next several days, we could still savor the memory of making cookies.

One day at cookie-making time, Lorinda arrived, invited by my daughter Dawn. She was starved for love. I could see it in her eyes. She had never made cookies before, a fact which astonished my children. A little more flour went on the floor, more icing dribbled down the counter. But the glow on Lorinda's face made it worthwhile. I made Lorinda her very own apron, which she wore like a badge of honor. The apron seemed to signal to her an acceptance as part of our family. I became "Mom".

My life went south. My husband left and money was scarce. I even had to go on food stamps (very humiliating). But I needed those cookie-making sessions as much as my children. It meant we were still connected.

The girls grew up and moved away. I re-married. Fourteen years into that marriage, we moved into a brand-new house. I had never had my own home before. It was a delight to fix it up. But there was that yellow bowl. I've never liked yellow. So, I bought a new set of nesting mixing bowls. Burgundy. I placed the new set in the yellow bowl on the shelf. Each time I opened that cupboard, the yellow bowl yelled at me. It had to go. But I just couldn't get rid of it. It was filled with too many memories.

My daughter, Lyn, came to visit. Of the three girls, she had been the one who wanted to make cookies the most. I took her to the cupboard, pointed to the yellow bowl and asked, "Would you like to have that bowl?" A grin from ear to ear was my answer.

And so, it went home with her. But that is not the end of the story.

She is in a relationship with a man who has a young son, Blake. He visits his dad every other weekend. Blake had never made cookies. Lyn could not let that happen. Out came the yellow bowl. A mess was made. But a glow was on the face of a young boy.

One weekend, plans had to be changed and Blake was not going to get to come for his visit. With tears in his eyes and a quiver in his lip, he said to his mother, "But I was going to make cookies with Lyn". Special arrangements were made for Sunday. He got to make his cookies. As he ate the dough, he loudly proclaimed to his dad "this is part of the tradition".

The yellow bowl is still doing its job, making memories.

The Saga of Marie

I missed out on having any grandparents. But I knew the kind of grandparents I wished for. Warm and loving, with lots of hugs and kisses to go around.

I grew up, married and had children of my own. But I had to live by a strict moral code with rigid rules and no wiggle room for "warm and loving". By the time I had gone through my metamorphosis and became a person with my own set of values, my children were too old to cuddle on my lap.

So, I waited for my first grandchild. I would be the grandparent I never had.

When I learned of a pending grandchild from my youngest daughter, it took me by surprise. The marriage took place, but the "father to be" was Canadian, so the new couple moved north of the border to live with his parents. Six months into the pregnancy, I got the phone call that my daughter was in labor. Sitting by the phone, crocheting on a baby afghan for my first grandchild, I waited all night.

Marie weighed 1120 grams at birth. I had no idea how much that was, so had to ask the nurse to convert it into pounds. 2 lbs. 7 oz. 12 inches long.

Tiny and fighting for her life.

She was transferred to a children's hospital in Vancouver, BC that specialized in preemies. That would be her home for the next 117 days. Then came the phone call telling us they planned to give her up for adoption. The trip north was made. Placing my hands through the rubber openings of the Isolette, I carefully touched my first grandchild. Would I ever see her again?

Raising the tiny preemie was just not a possibility for my husband and me. We had recently moved to a new town to start a business. I was working four jobs to make ends meet until we got on our feet.

Arriving back home, I called my brother to tell him the news. When he heard that we would not be taking the baby, he said he and his wife would. They immediately made contact with my daughter and her husband and were given the go ahead. They kept in constant touch with the hospital, and then flew halfway across the United States to get Marie when she was released.

Nine months later, the young couple decided they wanted her back. Thus, began the saga of Marie and her travels. By the time she was six, she had lived in two provinces in Canada, in Washington, California, Texas and Florida. She had lived with her parents, my brother and his wife, my other daughter, Lyn, several times, her mother and new husband and then some unknown people in Florida.

But her journey was not over.

Unmarried again, her mother became pregnant. She asked me to be her labor coach. I agreed. My husband and I helped my daughter and Marie travel from Florida to Washington.

I was present at my second grandchild's birth. I had high hopes.

And then my daughter placed Marie in a mental facility, took my grandson and moved, leaving no forwarding address.

My husband and I set aside an entire weekend to pray about the situation. Our finances had stabilized. But did we want to raise another child? Yet when we looked at Marie's future, we felt we had no choice. We went to court to gain temporary custody of Marie. That process was costly and took about a year. A year after that, Lyn moved to town. She was granted permanent custody.

There was no "warm and loving". Hugging Marie was just not an option. She was diagnosed with "Attachment Disorder". She had never bonded with another person. The diagnoses just kept coming. Aspergers. Bipolar. ADHD and on and on. She needed to be watched 24/7. Lyn and I "tag teamed".

I acquired a medical library, trying to understand what we were dealing with. Various medicines were prescribed. Some made her lips turn blue and she became a zombie. Others only escalated her behaviors.

It's the closest I have ever come to burnout.

Those were some of the roughest years of my life. I reached a whole new level of understanding about the wide scope of mental illnesses.

Honor Thy Mother

During the first 11 years of my life, my older brother was my "protector". But as he confessed years later, he had to care more about getting away than staying to protect. Being in the Navy was easier than living at home.

So, it was just the two of us: Mother and me.

Mother was not someone who gave love. She demanded instant obedience, confession and shame. The results were constant feelings of guilt and fear. I felt like I lived with a warden. Mother left wounds invisible to the eye. That all changed when I turned 15. Mother and our church arranged that I should marry the preacher's son. Before I completed high school, I married and moved away.

As I grew older and worked on me, I struggled to find good attributes about my Mother. Thoughts of her would turn negative almost immediately. The Ten Commandments were fairly easy to follow, except that fifth one. How could I "honor" my Mother?

Truly desiring to follow the Commandments, I began to research. I discovered that "honor" could also be defined as "love" or "respect". It could also mean "not rebelling against or challenging" her authority. I had that one down pat.

I began to dig in my memories for scraps of value in the way she raised me. Something I could respect, or at least feel good about.

One memory came to me. Eating ice cream. Together.

We were poor. Ice cream was a huge treat. On rare occasions, we would walk the six blocks to the grocery store, purchase a pint of ice cream, and walk home. Kansas gets hot in the summer. By the time we reached home, the ice cream had already softened.

She would place the brick shaped pint on the counter of the hutch in the room we called a kitchen. First, she opened the end flaps. Then she pried back the flap along the edge, laying the container out flat. With a knife, she divided the brick of ice cream in half, placing each half in a bowl. We would take our bowl and spoon, climb down the outside stairway and sit on the steps of the front porch below.

There was a proper way to eat ice cream. You scraped the soft ice cream off with your spoon and placed it in your mouth. While you savored that bite, you turned the brick over. The bottom side was now softened, so you scraped and ate it. This pattern continued until the ice cream was gone.

I felt close to my Mother while we ate our ice cream. She didn't talk.

Mother was into health before it was fashionable. Since we walked everywhere we went, she got her cardio. But daily she did exercises on the floor. She also would stretch her leg by walking up to the counter of the hutch, throw her leg up on it, and then bend over it.

Mother jumped rope. Her notoriety spread and she was given an assortment of jump ropes, some complete with bells and whistles. Any time she had a visitor, out would come the jump rope and she would exhibit her skills. When she reached 80, my sister decided "enough" with the jumping and took them all away.

A few years before her death, my husband and I went to visit Mother in Kansas. The temperature on her front porch said 112 degrees. She had never had air conditioning. But the trusty hassock fan was moving the hot air. As she greeted us at the door, her phone rang.

At age 83, she jumped over the fan on the way to answer it.

From my earliest memories of her, until the last time I saw her before her death, she told me her weight. It was always 140.

We took in washings and ironings for a living. But no matter where her money came from, whether earnings or from family, she tithed on it. On a regular basis, she demonstrated the "widow's mite" to me.

One memory I have that has allowed me to "honor" my Mother is the image I have in my head of her bent over her Bible, reading. She never missed a day. I admit, sometimes she beat me over the head with what she read, but she knew her scripture.

My Mother was one of the strongest people I have ever known. Even though her God seemed like an ogre to me, she received strength in her belief that sustained her through some very difficult times.

My Haven

For many children, the person in their life that makes them feel safe and loved is their mother. In my world, that wasn't true. My sister, Joan, was my haven. She was the only sibling who lived in the same town as my mother and me. Her husband, Lee, worked nights. So I spent many evenings at Joan's house. Her two daughters, Ann and Sara, became like sisters to me. Lee was the dad I never had.

Joan was obese. I've been with her when she broke a chair when she sat down. I've helped pull her from the bathtub when she was stuck. To the world, Joan was a jolly lady. But that laughter covered an inner pain that would not go away. I could sense the anguish in her silent moments. She never shared with me the cause of her torment.

As I think of her, the memories wash over me.

My mother and I did not have television. But Joan did. A small set that showed black and white. We would have "slumber parties" on the floor in front of that little box. Back then, the programs didn't need a rating system. They were all safe for children to watch. My favorites were "Alfred Hitchcock" and "The Twilight Zone". My mind worked on the details of those shows for days. Of course, we watched the standards too; "I Love Lucy" and "December Bride".

But not all evenings were spent on the floor. Many times, we gathered around the piano. Joan had a box of sheet music that had been given to her. We sang "Coming in on a Wing and a Prayer", "Ebb Tide" and "Stardust". We never made it to the bottom of the box in one evening.

Other times, she would get out the accordion and entertain us. I was fascinated as I watched her fingers fly up and down the buttons and keyboard. How did she get her two hands to do two different things at the same time?

When I married and moved away, Joan became my counselor and mentor. My husband said he wanted a roast for Sunday dinner. I had never had a roast and didn't know what it was. So, I called Joan. With her help, I made a pot roast that passed the "husband" test.

Pregnant with my first child, I was excited to tell my mother. The lecture began with "why would you bring another baby into this awful world?" and ended with the tales of enduring hours of extreme pain. I would be sorry I had chosen to give birth.

Crushed, I turned to Joan. Her excitement shone through. She loved babies. My mother's words disappeared as Joan painted an entirely different picture of pregnancy. She eagerly anticipated the first movements within me. Her face glowed as she talked of holding my child for the first time.

Then came the day she told me a secret. She was pregnant. At her age and weight, this was a life-threatening event. The first doctor told her she would have to abort the baby if she wanted to survive. So, she sought a second opinion and a third. She had to choose between her life and that of the unborn baby. An impossible decision to make.

A family counsel was held; Lee, Joan, Ann and Sara. They wanted their wife and mother to live. She acquiesced to their wishes. No one else knew why Joan was in the hospital briefly. Because I knew Joan so well, I knew she was dying inside. Therefore, it was no surprise to me when she told me, "I will not be alive on the day that I should have given birth".

I believed her. I just didn't know how she would accomplish it. The pregnancy had been kept a secret. Even though she lived next door to our mother, Joan's dilemma was never revealed to her.

One fall morning, my phone rang. My mother's voice told me Joan had died earlier that morning. Of heart failure. How true that was. At her funeral, her doctor expressed his condolences to me. But his next words caught me by surprise. "At least she died of natural causes". And so, I knew he knew she had not planned to live.

I miss her. I wonder what our relationship would have been like as two grown women. Would I ever have known the cause for her inner pain?

I loved her. She helped make me who I am today.

Popo and Nana

I met my in-laws when I was 12. Michael and Mae moved to our town to pastor our church. Of course, I didn't know then that they were destined to be my in-laws. I found that out when I was 15 and the church decided I should marry their son.

I liked Michael. He seemed nice and caring. Mae was very unusual. She ruled the household and Michael. "Yes, dear" were his most used words.

Right away, the church discovered that Mae didn't like the color of the parsonage, inside or out. She had Michael take the drapes down and carry them to the trash behind the church. When folks began arriving for church on Sunday, they saw the discarded drapes lying on the ground. The families who had no curtains took them home.

Next came the furniture. Again, the poor families took what they could use in their home.

When I "dated" their son, Ray, our dates consisted of attending church, eating Sunday dinner at his house, or spending Saturday evening watching television. It was at those Sunday dinners I learned about gossip. As we ate, Mae would tear apart what the congregation had said, worn, or looked like.

I learned hypocrisy in their home. One of the church's rules was "no television". It was "of the devil". The television antennas were the "devil's horns". So, imagine my surprise the first Saturday evening I was invited to Michael's house. Ray's bedroom was upstairs. Michael, Mae, Ray and I climbed the stairs, entered Ray's bedroom and the television was rolled out of the closet. We spent the evening reclining on the bed watching programs like "Gunsmoke". Before I left, the television had already been rolled back into the closet.

One thing I found very unusual about Mae was that she never got dressed. She spent the day in her thin negligee. That made me very uncomfortable.

Mae wanted a daughter. She found one in the child welfare system. The little girl was named Charlotte. The battle for custody of Charlotte went on for seven years. Mae finally won. Now she had a live dolly to dress fancy and play with. She changed her name from Charlotte to Kay. Mae sewed Kay frilly dresses, a new one each Sunday. Complete with hat and little white gloves, she put her on display.

Ray and I married and moved away. Occasionally Michael would have a meeting to attend and pay us a visit. He was very enjoyable to have as a guest. He was the dad I did not have.

Having Mae as a guest was a totally different story. She would arrive complete with white gloves. The doorsills, window tops and picture frames were given the "white glove test". Of course, I never passed.

When Ray and I had our first child, Mae made it very clear she was to be "Nana", never grandma and Ray would be "Popo".

I miscarried and Mae came to stay for awhile and "help". Yet it seemed I spent more time taking care of her than my children or myself. But I went too far when I suggested that the thermostat was set too low for the air conditioning. The children were cold.

Mae called her brother, who lived in the same town and ordered him to come get her. She was being mistreated. She stood in the driveway in the hot Oklahoma sun in her negligee, pillow in her arms and waited for him to come pick her up.

Then came the day Ray left me. I waited all night for him to come home. In the morning I called Michael and Mae to tell them I didn't know where their son was. Michael was on the phone with me, but I could hear Mae telling him what to say.

"Where did you think he would go when you kicked him out? Of course, he is here with us."

Then came the words that rocked my already unstable world.

"We never want to see you again."

Years later, at Thanksgiving time, when my children were gathered at my house, one daughter received a phone call telling her that Popo had died. Instantly his last words to me came to mind. Because of the turmoil in my life at the time, I had never grieved losing him. Now the tears flowed in buckets.

I decided it would be too awkward to go to the funeral, so I sent flowers "To the Only Dad I Ever Had".

Emotional Rollercoaster

Have you ever gathered around the toilet and had a funeral for a fish? If not, then you have not experienced life. Each daughter expressed their thoughts, a short prayer was offered and then we flushed, amid many tears.

Pets bring an abundance of joy, but then the loss is hard to bear.

We moved so often and so far across the country it was hard to keep a pet.

In Texas, a wooden doghouse was purchased. The children painted it red. The life of that dog was short, and the grief was unbearable when he expired due to an illness.

In Oklahoma, five-year old Dawn walked to the corner and back while I stayed in our yard with the younger two. Upon returning home, she held up her hand to show me her new pet. A black hairy tarantula. She wasn't allowed to keep it.

In Maryland, we had a black Cocker Spaniel named "Little Black Sambo", which was left behind when we moved back to Oklahoma.

For Christmas one year, two parakeets joined our family; Holly and Ivy. On occasion we would let them out to fly freely around the room, landing on the girl's heads and depositing at will. Not such a good idea.

When my husband left us in Nebraska, I thought a dog would help the children through the trauma. A white poodle named "Tiffany" became a member of our family. Even though she was designed to be the children's pet, she became valuable to me too as she sat by my side night after night as I grieved the loss of my marriage and faced an uncertain future.

One day Dawn, took Tiffany for a walk. I was busy in the kitchen when I heard her coming down the street, her wails preceding her. Tiffany had jumped out of her arms to chase a rabbit. Just as she ran across the street, a car came by. Dawn was absolutely traumatized.

A single mom, with three children to calm down, I sought help from a neighbor. I asked if he could help me retrieve the dog and bury it. You have to wonder about some people in the world. In front of the children he said, "Oh my goodness. There's no need to bury it. Just wrap it in a newspaper and throw it in the trash".

The wails grew louder.

I sought help elsewhere.

Lyn had more than one pet. Some of them she seemed to keep in her pockets, but others in her room. The most memorable one was "Jimmy", a water newt. Life became a little jittery when he would escape. But she loved him.

In Idaho, we acquired a darling "peekapoo" that was given to us by a lady in the church. A few weeks later, her son came to our door and took it back. He explained she gave it away as punishment to him. Now my children carried the pain.

After moving again, the girls adopted the squirrels that lived in the trees. Leaving peanuts on the little front stoop, they would watch from behind the screen door as the squirrels would climb the steps, pick up a peanut and make quick work of opening the shell and popping the peanut in their mouth. Eventually, the squirrels became so tame they ate out of their hands.

Dawn had a cat named "Sativa" that had a unique way to get to the basement from the main floor. She slid down the metal vent for the heating system. That screeching sound could be heard by the neighbors. It was especially enjoyable in the middle of the night.

The last pet we had before the children all left the nest was a Cocker Spaniel named "Toby". We had a delightful time with Toby. I had remarried. My husband, John, decided Toby needed a trim. He took Toby to the groomer. The groomer faced an impossible task, because Toby's fur was totally matted with cockle burs. So, she shaved him.

When John went to retrieve him, Toby would not look at him. Tail between his legs, he headed for the back yard and hid. He acted like he felt naked and embarrassed. And one thing was clear. Toby did not like John at all, for weeks. That man just couldn't be trusted.

Pets are expensive and sometimes destructive. It's like having another child around. But the wag of a dog's tail and the look of trust in its eyes make it all worthwhile.

Imposter in the Midst

The definition of "cousin" is: the child of your aunt or uncle. That would entail knowing either my mother's or my father's sisters or brothers. Never having met my father or anyone on his side of the family, that leaves him out. My mother had many siblings. In my early life, I met one of her brothers and three of her sisters, once.

I have no idea who their children are.

My three oldest sisters were pregnant at the same time my mother was expecting me. The same month of my birth, two nieces were born. Three months later I gained a nephew.

I grew up with my older sister's and brother's 13 children around me. I thought we were cousins.

I spent a lot of time with one of the nieces born the same month as me. Pictures taken in the early 1940's show us together at almost every family gathering. I was the one with the bows in my hair, one on each side of my head. She was the knocked-kneed one.

One vivid memory is of us scratching and biting each other in a wild fight. We ended up knocking a picture off the wall. The corner of the glass frame hit me on my elbow. Her father doctored me with something that looked like black tar and then sat us side by side against the wall to consider our behavior. I still carry the battle wound.

When I was 12, my older brother left me in charge of his three boys while he and his wife ran a lengthy errand. I placed a quilt on the front lawn for the baby and watched the other two as they played in the yard. After two hours, my brother returned to find his baby in the direct sun and turning pink. That baby is now a middle-aged, bald-headed man. When the family gathers, at least once the story must be told of why he is bald. I burned all his hair follicles.

Since two of my brother's-in-law were amateur photographers, many pictures were taken of the family. We were arranged in all types of groups; all the women, all the men, each family group, etc. Then it was time for the picture of all the cousins. Since I thought I was one, I would run to join them as they posed. Some adult in the family would escort me from the group. I didn't belong.

I looked like the cousins. I acted like the cousins. I was the same age as the cousins. Why wasn't I one? As I grew older, I began to understand that I was the "aunt". But I sure felt like a "cousin". Then came the day that the cousins rebelled. They would not have their picture taken without me in it. All the explaining went unheeded. I was one of them! In the midst of the pictures of the cousins, there is an imposter. The one with the bows on her head. But I had been accepted.

Where's Your Heart?

It's been said "home is where the heart is". My heart has sure been a lot of places.

118 S. Rural Street

22 West Street

714 Cottonwood Street

723 Sunnyslope Street

And then I turned 17 and married.

Three moves later, our first daughter, Dawn, was born. We brought her home to a metal Quonset hut provided by the college. When Dawn's father became a pastor, our next home was in the back of the church. On Sunday mornings, our bedrooms became Sunday School classrooms. Dawn's bedroom had little benches in it and her toys became the property of the church kids on Sunday.

But something went wrong, and we were given until sundown to get out of town. Our things were loaded on a farm truck and hauled to my mother's house. Our home became her front bedroom, with a path through the storage boxes. My husband, daughter and I slept in the one bed.

After a brief move to another city, we ended up back in that front bedroom. By then I was pregnant again. The bed was crowded. In my eighth month, we moved to Texas. Lyn was born in August. Before her first birthday, I was pregnant again. In my eighth month, we moved to Oklahoma. Rene' joined us in that parsonage.

It was hard for my heart to keep up with my homes. About the time I would get curtains made and begin to feel at home, we would move again.

We had a lovely home in North Carolina. Hardwood floors. Wooded lot. Little stream in the back yard. I thought I was home for sure. We were there less than a year.

Maryland was next. One of my neighbors was my brother and his family. I knew for sure I was home. Less than a year later, we were headed for Oklahoma again.

For awhile, we lived in a motel. It's hard to make curtains and feel at home there.

After two more moves in Oklahoma, it was time to try Nebraska. I had never lived in such a huge house. A basement and an upstairs. Front and back stairways. I hadn't even completed the unpacking before we moved to a different house.

My heart was getting tired.

One more move and then he was gone. I was a single parent.

Idaho was my choice to start over. Our first home was a one-bedroom apartment, almost exactly like the one I had started in years before. In the one bedroom we had two bunk beds. That way each one of us had our own space, small as it was.

Money was scarce. We ate on a card table. But this is when the "home" part started to kick in. Curtains were made. Games were played. Popcorn was eaten. Books were read. Walks were taken. My heart was definitely here.

I obtained a job at the college which offered housing. Our next move was to a two-bedroom duplex. I had the girls draw straws to see which one got the short one and had to share a room with me. But they didn't have to change schools for this move. We just had more space. And then the school offered me an actual house, complete with basement and upstairs. We each had our own bedroom. Once again, the girls didn't have to change schools.

I was home for sure! I promised them NO MORE MOVES. I certainly meant it when I said it.

My job skills had improved so much that I could begin to earn a livable wage. But that would entail moving to the next town 22 miles away. Dawn was ready to graduate from high school, so it really wouldn't affect her. But I hated to move the other two. I wavered back and forth. It was a tough decision. We had now lived in the same school district for five years. The girls had actually been able to make some friends.

Move again? As hard as it was, I decided yes. And life went on.

In all my many moves, I learned a huge lesson. The house is not the home. My home is where my heart is; with my family.

Thanks for the Memories

In my box of old pictures, I have a photo of my family that does not bring back any memories for me. I'm probably five years old. But all six of my brothers and sisters are gathered around a pole of some sort and there in the middle is our mother. I've been told by my brother that was a family reunion.

As I grew older, we held some BIG family reunions. With six brothers and sisters, and each of them married and having children, we were quite a group. Usually, at least one of the siblings could not make it and we would leave a hole in the picture for the missing one.

I will never forget the time the women were where they were supposed to be, in the kitchen getting the food ready. The men and children were in the living room. Suddenly the sound of a gun firing reverberated through the house. All food preparations were forgotten as we ran pell-mell for the next room.

My brother-in-law had been showing his hunting rifles to the kids. One went off. There was a hole in the ceiling. No one was injured. He got rid of his guns and never owned another.

During the years of my first marriage, attending family reunions just weren't necessary. Then came the lean years, when I did not have the funds to attend them.

When I married again, we had to work out a deal with our families. Alternate summers.

We traveled to Utah with our tent, to camp in the back yard of his cousin's house. The next summer took us to Colorado to my brother's house. We had a delightful time sitting in his back yard and viewing the Rocky Mountains.

My niece opened up her home in Idaho for a reunion. It was August and NASCAR was racing at the "Brickyard" for the first time. Some of the reunion took place outside and some inside, cheering for our favorite. My older brother did not want to know ANYTHING about the race. He was recording the race and would watch it in detail later.

One summer our destination was a park in northwestern Kansas, so Uncle Orrin could attend. He was very elderly and couldn't travel. Tape recorders were running as he related stories of the olden days. He died shortly after that visit. Some tents were flooded in the night when there was a tremendous thunderstorm. I felt semi-safe in the not-so-new little motel we were staying in. The wind blew pretty hard.

Then came the year my husband and I moved to our new house. When the talk began about when and where to have the next reunion for my side of the family, I was pretty adamant. It would be here, in my very first home of my own.

I had never done this before but charged ahead. We had friends who owned a breakfast and lunch restaurant. They opened on a Friday evening, just for our family. As I looked around those tables, my heart felt like bursting. They catered the food for us the next day, which was served in my very own back yard.

Family came from Washington, Oregon, Idaho, Colorado and Iowa. My nephew celebrated his 50th birthday, complete with cake and birthday hat.

I don't care much for posed pictures, but there was one I really wanted. In the corner of my back yard, I have a bench under a tree. I begged and pleaded for my two brothers to sit on that bench. Even though the picture was taken, the memory is far more vivid. My two brothers, in my back yard, sitting on my bench. I go to that bench regularly and visit them. Of course, they don't know that. (Or do they?)

Since both of my brothers have heart trouble, I was concerned about their health and wondered when (or if) I would see them again. Little did I know that I was seeing my sister-in-law for the last time. We met when she was nine, and I was far closer to her than my sisters. A very strong, stoic person, the last time I saw her she had tears in her eyes. She knew something I didn't. She had cancer. Before the year ended, she was gone.

The reunions don't come so often anymore. Life is different these days. The older ones are all gone. I only have two brothers left.

But I'm so glad for the memories.

Texting Queen

I don't enjoy talking on the telephone. Maybe it's because we didn't have one until I was in grade school. Or perhaps I had no need for one. No friends. Besides, I'm sure the religious culture I grew up in had talking on the phone labeled as some kind of a sin. Then when I married, I was still not allowed to have friends. Same religion. Probably same sin.

I just wasn't used to talking on the phone.

New marriage. New Christian perspective. I was allowed to use a telephone whenever I wanted. But a land line worked just fine for me. If someone called while I was gone, they left a message on the answering machine. Most of the time that did not entail a return call.

As my children moved away, talking on the phone became a necessity. Only because I love them dearly, will I stay on the phone past 15 minutes. One hour is pretty much my absolute max, no matter how much love there is.

A computer was purchased for me, and my new favorite way of communicating became email. I said what I wanted to say and then I was through.

Then cell phones came along. Why would I want a phone to go every where with me? When my husband, John, took me to the "phone" store, I told them I just wanted a basic phone. No gadgets. My "new gadget lover" husband wanted all the bells and whistles.

When it was time to renew our phone contract, they no longer carried just basic phones. You had to have the extras. We worked out a deal. For a credit on our contract, they gave me the phone that you buy the minutes for as you go.

Now that we each carried our phones with us, did we really need a land line? After much discussion, we cancelled our home phone. That meant I really did need to carry a phone with me. But that didn't mean I had to like it.

So, imagine my surprise, January 2nd, 2008, when John came home with two boxes, each containing an iPhone. He ripped his box open and was immediately consumed with the "new gadget". I eyed the other box suspiciously.

"Don't open that box unless I say so", I told him. We could always return it. Why would I need an iPhone?

For over a week, I pondered that little box. I watched John as he used his. I did some research online. I knew enough about computers to know that there would be a huge learning curve to use that little gadget. Did I really want to go to all that trouble?

Late one Friday afternoon, I said, "Ok, open the box." We sat on the couch, side by side, learning together. This phone had a "text" option. That was new to me. John explained it was kind of like "instant messaging". The shrug of my shoulders told him he was talking a foreign language.

The plan he had purchased allowed 200 texts per month. No problem.

Sitting side by side, we texted each other. I was getting the hang of it. So, I sent a text to a daughter. A few minutes later, the phone made a little "ding" and I had an answer from her. Maybe this could work. We were still "learning" at 1:30 a.m. Finally, we called a halt to the whole thing and went to bed.

As the days progressed, instead of a quick phone call to tell a member of my family something, I just typed out a few little words and hit "send".

I DID NOT HAVE TO TALK ON THE PHONE!

One of the most hilarious moments in these past few months was when we received our first phone bill. I had gone over the limit in "texting". But I was hooked. I took myself down to the "phone" store and signed up for the next level of texting, 1,500 texts per month, instead of only 200.

At age 65, I had become the "texting queen".

In June, I took a car trip, driving over 1,400 miles. When I would stop to buy gas, eat, or take a picture, a little text to John kept him posted of my progress. Other texts went out to the daughters I was traveling to meet. And I didn't have to talk on the phone to keep them informed of my progress.

So far, I haven't gone over 1,500 texts in one month.

Simplifying

My husband sits beside me on the couch. Objects keep flying by his head. Finally he turns to me and asks, "What are you doing?"

My answer, "I'm simplifying".

I have a plan. I bring a pile of papers, magazines, or other stuff. I place the pile in my lap and then I simplify. Whatever is no longer necessary in my life, I fling toward the back door. The "keepables" are placed in proper stacks on the floor so they can be put away in their respective places.

During one of these flinging episodes, I heard a little voice quietly say, "I hope I'm still necessary in your life."

I've reached that age when it is time to focus on the time I have left. All the unnecessary and peripheral things need to go.

I plan to be a "late bloomer". Some flowers in my garden bloom in the spring, some in the summer and then some in the fall. I was robbed of my springtime by an overzealous religious church and mother. In late summer I began to sprout and grow. Now it's time to produce those fall flowers in my life.

That takes focus.

First I have to decide just exactly where I need to expend my energies. I've discovered that God has given me gifts; gifts He intended me to use to help others. Who can I help? What kind of help can I give them?

Next, I need to equip me for that ministry. What do I need to learn? How do I need to change?

And then there is always the fear.

To enable me to better help others, I felt God leading me to a group called Toastmasters, an organization designed to help you learn how to do public speaking. But the fear kept me captive for six years, frozen in my ineptitude. Only God could have helped me master that fear, show up at a Toastmaster's meeting and then join the club. That meant I had to participate by giving speeches. I no longer cry. But the fear is there, lurking just below the surface.

What about the fear of rejection? I put words on paper. What makes me think someone else wants to read them? Am I being arrogant? I push past those thoughts and submit an article to "Faithwriters".

As I focused on my next step, I knew I needed to be organized to accomplish anything. So when my husband took an 11-day motorcycle trip, my plan kicked in. The day he left town, I moved everything that was movable out of my office. This made a big mess in the living room. It was the price I had to pay.

Once again, I began the process of simplifying. There was no flinging this time, just sorting through files, books, papers and office stuff. Slowly I am re-building my office. The re-organizing enables me to think better.

To allow me more time to focus on God's leading, I have backed off in my hours at work. Except for emergencies, I plan to work only Monday through Wednesday.

So here I sit. Just exactly what is it I'm getting ready for? I don't know!

I'm taking this a day at a time, a prayer at a time, a new concept at a time. I have no idea how many years I have left, but God does. He knows exactly what it is He wants me to accomplish with them.

Maybe I'll be another "Grandma Moses" and come into my prime in my 80's.

The process of simplifying removes the unnecessary to enable me to focus on the necessary: people. After all, people are the only thing that really matter.

When I stand before the Bema, I will not be asked what name was on the church I attended or how much money I had in the bank. The kind of clothes I wore or the house I lived in will have no importance. As my life passes in review, the focus will be on my interactions with people; each one as they came across my path. Will anyone be in heaven because of me?

So as I live each day, I focus on people. The simplifying process carries over into each conversation. The unnecessary must be sorted out and thrown away. To discover the real treasure in each person, I do a little mental "flinging", discarding the peripheral words and actions and focusing on the "keepable" traits.

God is teaching me to love others. That's the plan for now.

The Consequence

Even though I had been given explicit instructions by my husband that I was not to attend my sister Joan's funeral, I was mentally getting ready to go anyway. Only my love for Joan made me willing to suffer the consequences.

I waited until the next morning. Trying to keep the routine the same as usual, I fixed his breakfast, sent him off to work and the two older girls off to school. The youngest, Rene', would have to go with me. Quickly I packed a suitcase and took it to the car. With my heart pounding, I placed the phone call.

"Ray, I just wanted to let you know I am going to Joan's funeral. You will need to pick up Dawn and Lyn after school".

His reply was exactly as expected. "I told you you weren't going. She's dead and gone and that's a fact. Now just forget about it."

"But, Ray, I really need to go. She was like my mother."

Having never gone against his orders like this before, I didn't know how to handle it. I longed for him to understand my need.

Laughing, he replied, "Just how do you plan to get there? I told you I'm not taking you."

"I plan to drive."

"You'll never make it. You probably don't even know how to start the car. Now forget it."

I couldn't.

My time was limited. He could be home in ten minutes. I hung up the phone and ran to the car, Rene' bouncing on my hip. Even though he didn't allow me to drive, I did know how. It was Joan's husband, Lee, who had taught me.

I drove south over the state line as fast as the speed limit would allow, keeping one eye on the rear-view mirror. The tears running down my cheeks matched the rain pouring down on the car. Joan had been my light in a very dark life. And now she was gone. I had to say goodbye.

When the family gathered at the funeral home, imagine my surprise to see Ray, Dawn and Lyn walk through the doorway. He kept a tight grip on the girl's hands and never glanced in my direction. But he smiled and hugged his way through the family to find seats. He was there again at the graveside, head bowed, never releasing his hold on Dawn and Lyn. And then he was gone.

Lee was so distraught I agreed to stay two more days. Joan was only 42… too young to die. Lee paced the floor. He didn't sleep. He needed help. So, I asked him if he would like to go home with me. We had a six-bedroom, three-level house. He could stay as long as he needed. He agreed.

He did the driving going home, following my directions to my house. We walked up on the front porch. The drapes were open. Even before I got to the door, I could see no one lived there. The house was empty.

Now I understood what my consequence was.

I didn't know where I lived. I had no idea if they were still in the same town… or if I was homeless. With Lee standing beside me, I felt about three inches tall. I had no idea if there would be a place for him. How humiliating! What if I did find them and he wouldn't let me in? Where were the girls? What was I supposed to do now?

Eyes downcast and fear clenching my heart, I walked to the neighbor's house and rang the doorbell. She thought it was hilarious he had moved and not told me where. I didn't see the humor. But she did know the address.

We pulled up in front of the house at the new address. We walked up on the porch and rang the doorbell. Ray came to the door, smiling and friendly.

"Come on in. Good to see you, Lee." Ray guided Lee through the living room, dining room and into the kitchen. "So sorry about Joan. You are welcome to stay with us as long as you like."

I stared at the furniture and curtains, the lamps, dishes in the china hutch. I could see our appliances in the kitchen. Not a box in sight. Everything was put away. I had no idea where anything was.

How had he done this?

My disobedience and his move were never mentioned. He acted like we had always lived there.

And life went on.

The Good Wife

When we moved from Maryland to Oklahoma, a motel room became our temporary home. Day after day I sat in that room with Rene', our youngest daughter. Dawn and Lyn were in school. Ray, my husband, could not seem to find a house. And I wasn't feeling well.

Ray's life, however, was a different story. He had a plush office in a tower building with a deck and view of the city. He was climbing the corporate ladder rapidly.

Finally, a house was selected. I began the task of making it a home. But I was making constant trips to the bathroom. After one episode I felt turned wrong side out and needed to hang onto the sink for support. That's when I spied the red color in the toilet bowl. I was bleeding!

Now what to do? I wasn't to bother Ray. He was just getting started with his new job. I was scared and wanted someone to care. But Ray was the only adult I knew in town.

When Ray arrived home that night, I apologized for the lack of work I had accomplished that day and then explained my reason. With a wave of his hand, he discharged me and asked what there was for supper. I persisted, which I rarely did. I wanted to see a doctor. Something was wrong. Ray calmly explained his insurance hadn't gone into effect yet and he wasn't going to spend his money to take me to a doctor.

I was no better the next day. Something was drastically wrong, and I needed professional help. I mentioned it to Ray again. He had had enough. If I would promise to hush about it, he would take me to a doctor. But after only a brief examination and a few questions, the doctor explained I needed to be hospitalized. I tried to tell him my husband would never go for that. He thought I was joking.

As I sat in the examining room, I heard their voices reverberating from the waiting room. A totally bewildered doctor returned to me, telling me to get dressed and go home. With a touch to my shoulder (which was like an electric shock because no man was supposed to touch me) he assured me he wouldn't just let this go. He would do something.

After leaving the doctor's office, we drove around while Ray made sure I understood that this issue was to be dropped. I would not be going to a hospital.

He said, "Now we are going to go home, so act like you're ok."

I tried desperately to hear somewhere in all his words that he cared about what was happening to me. But why would he? I was only his wife. We returned home with big smiles on our faces. There were no problems.

The next morning, the phone rang. It was my doctor. He explained he had reserved a hospital bed for me, and I was to check in by 2:00. When I told him I had no way to get there, he laid out a plan for me. Ask one neighbor to watch the children and then another to take me to the hospital. We were both aware that Ray was not an option. Who knew what his reaction would be? The only assurance I had was that the doctor was on my side.

Day after day I lay in the hospital bed. I was exhausted. Hospital tests can deplete your strength, especially when you are in short supply already. In his anger, Ray had not been to visit me once. I was alone.

A new face, a specialist, now smiled down at me. He told me what he believed to be my physical problem. I would be on a special diet and medication for the rest of my life; possibly be able to prevent further deterioration and repeated surgeries.

He said, "I don't know what you are keeping inside of you and not telling anyone, but it is killing you. You need to find someone to talk to". Then he left.

I knew what he meant.

But a good wife did not question her husband. A good wife did not ever say I don't think you should do that. And certainly, a good wife would not seek counseling and tell anyone else any of her husband's actions that were disturbing her.

I was a good wife.

Medicine was prescribed. The neighbor took me home. The pretense continued.

The Wisdom of Mac

Growing up, it had been made very clear to me that I was to do as instructed and never question God, the pastor or anyone in the church, or my mother. So, when I was told at the age of 15 that I would be marrying the preacher's son, I remained silent. In that marriage, my total compliance to my husband's authority cost me my health, but I remained true to my teachings.

After my husband left me, I began to work on a "new" me. I took my three daughters and moved to a state where we had never lived to begin a "new" life. Old programming dies hard. Even though the denomination I had devoted my whole life to had kicked me out when my husband left, that is the church the girls and I walked to on that first Sunday morning.

But they had no class for a divorced 30-year old woman. The Associate Pastor escorted me down a hall and tried to usher me into a room full of older ladies, some with blue hair. I turned to that pastor and asked, "Would you want to go in there?" He explained they had no class for me.

So, he suggested I try a class that met across the street in a house. Unknown to me, that class was known to others as the "renegade" class because they questioned everything. Unknown to that pastor, he was sending someone who had never challenged any dogma of the church into a room filled with uninhibited minds. What an eye opener!

Some Sundays I feared the roof would fall in. Other Sundays I would find myself thinking if possibly they could be right about an issue. Just even allowing such thoughts was frightening. But these were college professors and professional people. Obviously, they were smart.

Over time I began to offer a few tidbits of my life. One Sunday the topic was on anger. To me it was simple. Anger was a sin. Therefore, you should never be angry. And I never had.

After class, Mac (a psychologist) laid his hand on my shoulder. I flinched. Being touched by another man was against my programming. He saw the stiffening but did not remove his hand.

"I've been watching you," he said. "If anyone else said they had never been angry, I would laugh. But I believe you when you say it. And you've had some things happen to you that you should be angry about. I would like to help you learn how to be angry."

My response. "I'm sorry, but I don't want to learn to be angry. Anger is a sin."

"No," he said. "It's what you do when you are angry that is the sin."

I'd never heard it that way before.

"But I can't afford any sessions with you", I told him.

He smiled as he said, "I would not charge you. It would be my pleasure to help you out of your box."

I had no clue what that meant. But I liked Mac, so agreed to a time and place.

My new routine was to go to work, go to Mac's and then go home. I would walk through a living room in disarray, stepping over three children watching television, go immediately to the kitchen and begin to cook supper. After about the third session with Mac, I came home, walked through the living room and headed for the kitchen. Suddenly, I did a U-turn. Striding to the television, I turned it off and stood in front of it. Three pairs of very wide eyes stared at me, not sure what to do.

"I've been going to Mac to learn how to be angry, and I'm very angry," I said in a calm and level voice. "Now get up off your butts. Dawn, you do this and this.

Lyn, you do that and that. Rene' you take care of this and that. And I'm giving you fair warning. When I come home from work, the house will be clean. You will also learn to cook your own supper. Now go."

As I walked toward the kitchen, my step was lighter. I had just been angry. It felt good.

The Breath of Life

The question of when life actually begins is everywhere in the political news these days. Since I have been present at the bedside for four of my grandchildren's births, I do know that the drama of each one of their lives began before their first breath.

Rene' called me early one Sunday morning to tell me it was time. Over the next few hours, I encouraged, coached, and supported her as she worked her way through the process. I saw the head appear and just that quickly I knew we were in trouble. I've never seen anyone move as swiftly as the doctor did in that moment. As he said, "We have a problem", his thumbs moved to each side of Alex's neck and under the cord that was wrapped there.

Alex had not taken his first breath and was already failing in the "Game of Life".

I watched as they gave him his Apgar test. Two out of a possible ten. Anything below five is life threatening. They rushed him from the room to continue working on him.

After such a critical beginning, he is now alive, well and 15 years old.

Having been present at one birth, I was an old hand at it. When Anne began labor, once again I stood by the bedside. But I knew too much. I watched the monitors. I saw the baby's heartbeat drop precariously low. Taking my husband, John, to the hallway, I told him I thought there was a problem.

Within minutes the doctor made the pronouncement that the baby was in danger and they were going to do an emergency C-section. Richard was not outside the womb yet, but life was already dealing him a losing hand.

And again, the crisis passed. Richard will soon be a teenager, having no memories of those scary moments.

Four years later, all went smoothly as Anne labored to produce a daughter, Katherine. On that Monday, the cord was cut by the very proud daddy. Perhaps this time, she had been dealt a winning hand.

Taking 24 hours to make sure everything was ok; John and I got in our car and drove the five hours home. Checking in with the little family on Wednesday, I was told Anne was not feeling well. Instant red flag. When I asked to talk with her on the phone, my adrenaline kicked in. Holding the cordless phone to my ear, I pulled out a suitcase and began packing as I talked.

"You must call an ambulance. You need to get to the hospital NOW", I told her.

This time, it was the new mother that had been dealt the bad hand. She could not get her breath.

John and I drove over the speed limit through the night. Arriving at the hospital, we were told Anne was in Intensive Care. And the new baby? Since Katherine had been discharged, she could not be re-admitted. She would now live in the waiting room with the family.

Anne was placed on a respirator. The family tag-teamed in the waiting room, taking turns with the newborn. After three days of holding Katherine, I finally made special arrangements to get one of the carts they put the babies in when they are in the nursery. At least now we could lay her down.

Just as quickly as Anne's lungs had filled, they reversed direction and began to clear up. After five days, the tube was removed, and she was going to live.

You just never know with the "Game of Life".

Today Katherine is a very alive and well nine-year old.

Five years later, we received the phone call that labor had commenced. Again, we drove the five hours and got to the house just as Anne was headed to the hospital. The process seemed uneventful. But in those critical moments when the head appeared, I could tell something was wrong.

Jon was a fully formed little boy, still partially inside and connected to Anne with the cord. But the doctor was telling Anne not to push. (Did he even understand what he was asking?) Jon was covered with meconium. Before he breathed in for the first time, he needed to be suctioned to make sure his lungs could function. As the medical staff worked on Jon, they held back his actual moment of becoming a living, breathing soul!

The "Game of Life" is a roller coaster ride from before the first breath until that very final one.

Bethlehem Village

When my husband and I moved to our new home, I had Christmas plans for the living room with the 20-foot ceiling. Now I could finally have my adult, color-themed, elegant Christmas tree. I could already see it, in shades of burgundy and cream.

Since we moved in during November and my first order of business was to make a wedding dress, I didn't get to have my Christmas tree that year. But I began planning ahead. I purchased burgundy velvet ribbon and cream colored satin. The balls were burgundy and cream colored. The lights were all white. A string of pearls winding through the branches gave it a touch of elegance.

I had to stand on a step ladder to complete the decorating. An angel with a burgundy dress, holding lighted candles in her hands, was placed on the top of the tree. It was finished and looked just like I planned.

But somehow, it was not nearly as rewarding as I had expected. Sort of empty.

As I contemplated my feelings, I thought of previous Christmas trees. As a child, just my mother and me, we did not really decorate for Christmas. One of my first recollections of a Christmas tree involved a small clear plastic one, about ten inches high. It seemed rather bare as it sat on the metal trunk by the window. It was years later that I discovered the points on the ends of all the branches were supposed to have gum drops on them.

I recalled the first Christmas after my husband left. My three daughters and I waited until the "sale" at the Christmas tree lot and then brought home our "Charlie Brown" tree. The fun that year was making the ornaments. I had purchased a kit of wooden shapes that were awaiting paint. Spreading newspapers on the table, the children gathered around while I laid out the various paints and brushes.

Those ornaments became a mainstay on our tree each year. Each child could point with pride to the ones they had personally painted. After the children were grown and gone, I divided up those wooden ornaments and gave each of them a few of their masterpieces.

One year a member of the singles group at the church invited us to his home in northern Idaho the weekend before Christmas. "Home" was a small trailer where his parents lived in near poverty. But they had a lot of love to go around. Excitement was in the air as we headed into the woods to pick out a tree that would be chopped down in front of our very eyes, loaded on top of the car and driven back to our apartment. What a treat that had been.

Looking again at the elegant tree in my living room, I knew it was missing something. Children.

I kept my burgundy and cream decorations for a few years, but slowly my focus was changing. Our first year in the house, my friend had given me a ceramic lighted church, part of a Christmas village. Each year, my village grew.

Then came the year I chose the village over the Christmas tree. The village had grown so large that it filled the whole floor space of the living room. It was crowding out the tree. And I liked it!

My carefully planned burgundy and cream decorations were taken to Goodwill. The village took on a life of its own. I even named it; Cottonwood. It was fun to build. I would borrow children from the neighbors or bring in some school kids to help put it up. We would top off the evening with hot chocolate.

One year I sat and pondered the size of the village. It had grown to be ten times bigger than my nativity. Where, exactly, did I want my focus?

So I put out the word. Back off on the village additions. My new plan was to create a Bethlehem village.

A few pieces at a time, I began to build my Bethlehem village. Of course it has Anne, Joseph and the baby. The shepherds and lambs have gathered. The kings are presenting their gifts. But I also have a little drummer boy and a flute player. A young girl is holding her goose. Dogs lay at the feet of their masters. Horses nibble at hay in their shed. So far, I have added enough to Bethlehem to fill the dining room table.

And I don't miss a Christmas tree.

Traditions Old and New

It's funny how some holiday traditions get started. I had no idea when I began my unique idea for the holiday meal, that years later it would still be a "tradition".

As a single mom with three children, money was scarce. So I tried to do extra, inexpensive things to make the holiday more memorable. My plan was to provide the meat (usually a turkey from the Salvation Army). I sat the girls down and explained they would have a part in deciding the menu. I wanted each of them to choose a favorite food to go with the main dish.

We have had some unbelievable combinations for our celebration. Macaroni and cheese complete with ketchup, chicken and noodles and many other variations. We usually tried to invite a guest who had no place to go for the meal. As they looked in astonishment at the assortment before them, the "tradition" would have to be explained again.

Then it got even weirder. Boyfriends and then husbands would come to celebrate with us. Before I had a chance to say "enough", my kids had already explained to them that they got to choose a dish. When baked spaghetti squash was requested, I hurried to the computer and looked up how to cook it.

In the middle of all these years, I re-married. My husband, John, wrote the wedding vows out, gave them to me to edit (the word obey was not there) and then we had our ceremony. However, he failed to mention what he expected as part of my commitment. He had heard of our "tradition". His choice was oyster dressing, with the recipe written in his ex-wife's handwriting. He assured me it was part of my wedding vows.

I don't like fish. They are slimy and stink. Oysters are the worst of all. The first year, I wasn't even sure how to buy them. I discovered they come in a jar. I carefully followed my predecessor's instructions. But she failed to mention how small to make the pieces of oyster. So I cut them up into little chunks. I thought they would go down easier.

Wrong. Please, next year, make the oyster pieces bigger.

Each year I followed the hand-written recipe and made the oyster chunks larger. Finally, after several years of trying to get it right, John said, "Just don't cut them up at all. Leave them whole." How gross!

Oyster dressing truly was a gift of love. I couldn't seem to wash the slime off my hands, and I carried the odor of oysters for hours. And he was the only one who liked it! But it was his chosen dish. No complaining.

A long-standing tradition involved the making of Christmas cookies. We made all kinds. Snickerdoodles were rolled in red and green sugars. Candy cane cookies were time consuming to make. Half the dough had to be mixed with red food coloring. Then a white strip and a red strip of dough had to be twisted with the top curved down, to make a cane. While they were baking, the peppermint pieces were broken up to drop on the hot canes from the oven, melting the peppermint into the dough.

Of course we made sugar cookies cut in various shapes and frosted in red and green and covered with sprinkles and sugars. The wonderful fragrance of cookies lingered in the house for days.

Then came the years of the Atkins diet. No more old tradition. The turkey could remain, but scalloped potatoes and my home-made angel rolls were a thing of the past. Instead of potato salad, we had "unpotato" salad, replacing the potatoes with cauliflower. Deviled eggs could stay, but the green bean casserole was no more. I baked some kind of a sweet potato casserole. Dessert was layers of Jell-O and low-fat yogurt or pumpkin pie without a crust.

Now it is just the "two of us". And Atkins is still with us. So last year we made reservations to partake of the holiday brunch at the Red Lion. When word got out that we were eating alone, one of our "Starbucks Gang" friends would have none of that. We were invited to spend the day at his cabin in the mountains with his family.

Our contribution was a flower arrangement.

What a delightful time! Snow on the ground; so much that we got stuck. Entering the cabin, we were greeted by old friends and new. The aroma of a holiday meal filled the air.

Just like home.

Is It Christmas Yet?

Whatever happened to Thanksgiving? It's not even Halloween and the Christmas decorations, wrapping paper and cards have been on the store shelves for weeks.

When my children were young, we had a rule at our house. Christmas came AFTER Thanksgiving. There would be no Christmas music until then. Since I had raised them to act intelligent and ask questions, I then had to define exactly what I meant by "after Thanksgiving". I settled on "after the Thanksgiving meal is celebrated and the dishes cleared away".

Out would come the audiotapes, mostly Christian themed. But we had Charlie Brown and the Chipmunks. The "oldies" such as White Christmas and Rudolph were included. The music would start in the morning before school and begin again as soon as school was over. We had them all memorized and as the girls grew older; we would harmonize along with the songs.

The anticipation for Christmas grew daily.

The first Christmas after their father left, I was in despair. How would I provide anything for Christmas? The Salvation Army escorted me into a room full of games and toys and told me to pick one for each child. How grateful I was to be able to have a surprise for them on Christmas morning.

One year I gave them an Advent calendar, with a piece of chocolate hidden behind a flap for each day. As the countdown toward Christmas continued, the chocolate disappeared. They were supposed to take turns. Apparently one of them (unnamed of course) decided to eat the chocolate for the correct day and then have an extra counting back from the 25th. It wasn't pretty the day the flap was opened, and it was empty; from there until the end of the calendar.

That didn't work.

So I sewed an Advent calendar. Nothing edible. Just little pockets for each day, with a little present to place in the pocket to show that day had arrived. As far as I know, no one ate any of the presents.

Another rule at my house was regarding the amount of toys and games my children had acquired over the past year. Their father, my ex-husband, flooded them with presents on a regular basis. They needed to learn to share. A few weeks before Christmas, out would come a cardboard box. They knew the drill. They were to go through their toys and games and divide; one for them, one for the needy. The one for the needy had to be in good condition with all its parts and pieces.

They would accompany me as we took their spoils to the Salvation Army, to help someone else enjoy Christmas. We had been on that "needy" side and understood the gratefulness when gifts had been provided for us. It was time to give back.

We always decorated the tree early enough to enjoy it for at least a week. It was a big production. Christmas music playing, hot chocolate and cookies available in the kitchen, and usually a friend or two to help in the process. I enjoyed watching their deliberations for the perfect place for each item. I tried to just stay out of it, even though all the red bulbs might be on one side and all the lights on the other. Decorating the tree was about family and making memories.

The atmosphere changed for Christmas Eve. After attending the Christmas Eve service at the church, we would gather around the tree, sitting on the floor. I would read the Christmas story from Luke in the King James Version of the Bible. As they grew older, they had heard it so many times that we just quoted it. After some serious talking about the meaning of Christmas, then the mood would lighten. That's when we would say (from memory) "Twas the Night Before Christmas".

Christmas morning was especially hard on them. As early as 3:00 or 4:00 a.m., they would come to my bed and ask if it was Christmas morning yet. It was a trick. They knew it was morning and it was Christmas. If I said, "Yes", then we would all have to get up. But I was smarter than that. Another rule was given. It had to be light outside. As the first streaks of dawn appeared in the sky, the announcement would be made loud and clear. IT WAS CHRISTMAS MORNING!

The children are grown and gone. The Christmas season isn't nearly as action packed and chaotic. It's also a bit boring.

Inner Joy

Have you ever tried to help small children untangle strings of Christmas lights? By the time you have the strings in a straight line ready for decorating, you would rather just throw them down and go read a book. It takes a special kind of parent to prevail. Then come the years when the children get selective. The lights need to be all white, or blinking, or have little bubbles in them that move upward as they shine.

All too soon, the children are gone. You have plenty of time to untangle the lights by yourself. It's just not the same.

My husband, John, and I own a business. Since it involves people's healthcare and insurance, we get busier and busier toward the end of each year, as they try to use their insurance coverage. This makes for some very long days and nights. The rush is over by Christmas, and there is a huge lull until after New Years.

One year we traveled to Texas to visit my brother and his wife between Christmas and New Years. The flight had its problems and we arrived late and very tired. One of us was more tired than the other. The next evening, my brother loaded us all in his van and drove us around the Dallas area to look at the Christmas lights.

John promptly went to sleep. At first he was just emitting gentle noises. But as the tour of the lights continued, the noises grew louder. Soon, the entertainment was inside the vehicle instead of outside. When our laughter finally woke him up, we called it a night and went home.

John and I had never decorated the outside of our house, so one year we splurged and bought strings and strings of outside lights to put on our pine trees in the front yard. We worked for several hours, getting them just right. And then we waited for darkness so we could view our handiwork.

When the sunlight had faded, we eagerly switched on our Christmas lights. How beautiful! Job accomplished, we returned to the house and closed the door. About an hour later, I looked out the bedroom window and the trees were all dark. What had gone wrong? Our investigation led to the conclusion that the wires had been cut. No outside Christmas lights for us.

We never tried again.

Have you ever thought about the Christmas lights on that first Christmas? In Luke 2, it talks about an angel of the Lord appearing to the shepherds. The radiance of the Lord's glory surrounded them. Just how bright do you think that was? And then suddenly that angel was joined by a vast host (too many to count) of others. No wonder the shepherds were terribly frightened.

Those radiant beings were the world's first Christmas lights.

In Matthew 2:2 it talks about a star that rose in the sky, bringing wise men to Jerusalem in search of a newborn King. Then in verse 9 it says, "Once again the star appeared to them, guiding them to Bethlehem. It went ahead of them and stopped over the place where the child was". Verse 10 says, "When they saw the star, they were filled with joy!"

Perhaps it was just as some say; a conjunction of Jupiter, Saturn, and Mars. Or just maybe God created a special star designed for this first Christmas night. According to the notes in my Bible, the wise men (astrologers) traveled thousands of miles following that particular star. It sounds like a very unique Christmas light.

Today it seems neighbors are in a competition to see who can have the most lights on their house and in their yard. That battle carries over to the inside of the house. The trees viewed through the windows are loaded with many varieties of lights. Mantels, window ledges and stairway railings are included in the contest for the brightest display. Even though it seems a bit much to me, I say, "Go for it, if you can afford the electric bill".

Just as the wise men were filled with joy when they saw the star, we need to have an inner joy when we see the Christmas lights. They only represent what needs to be a greater focus on the core reason for the season.

It's time to worship the King.

The Personal Touch

Back in the "old" days, before scrapbooking became so popular, my mother made Christmas scrapbooks. Since we didn't receive very many greeting cards ourselves, our church congregation helped with her projects by collecting cards they received and then giving them to my mother instead of throwing them away.

At Christmas time, we would come home from church with a sack of cards. I knew what was coming next. My job was to cut out the pictures on the front of the Christmas cards. This was no easy task. I was to leave a narrow white border around the edge of the picture to help set it off when it was pasted in the scrapbook. By the end of a cutting session, I had grooves in my thumb and fingers from the grip I had on the scissors.

Never was I allowed to do any pasting. She was the master of that. When the scrapbook was full, then it magically disappeared from my life. I have no idea what she did with them.

But to this day, I have a hard time throwing away Christmas cards. As I type these words, the cards from last year are laying right here beside me, in preparation for this year's sending and receiving. I will take one more look through the assorted accumulation before finally discarding them. Every year the pile gets a little smaller.

In my first marriage, I was obligated to send Christmas cards to anyone I may have met briefly on the street. I recall sending out 200 one year. With today's postage rates, that would be costly.

As the children grew older, they were each given a box of cards so they could send them to their friends. Writing in and addressing Christmas cards was a whole day project, complete with music and hot chocolate.

Each year I send fewer than the year before. On top of last year's cards are two boxes of new Christmas cards. With 30 cards to a box, right now it seems I'm sending out 60 this year. I try to buy early to get the ones that actually mention the reason for Christmas on them.

My plan has always been to write something creative and personal to each recipient. But the busy season arrives abruptly and I never seem to accomplish that. And now the new trend is sending Christmas newsletters. I have a bad attitude about those newsletters. It seems to me they are more of a "bragging" newsletter. Sometimes I don't even read them; all typed, bordered and impersonal. I just glance at the signature. One handwritten sentence would be preferable.

I've been doing my own little survey about Christmas cards and who sends them. Some people actually don't do Christmas cards any more. Others only send to people that don't live in the same town with them, since they see the local people all the time. Others send to only family.

Each year, for over 40 years, the first card I received was from Nina Weidner. She was my neighbor as a child back in Kansas. She had a daughter my age, Jeannette. But Jeannette had cerebral palsy and was confined to a wheelchair. I became Jeannette's best friend.

Even though I married and moved away, I still kept in touch with Nina. When I had my first child, I visited her. As I proudly laid my little girl in her arms, the tears slowly rolled down her cheeks. She was so delighted. Then I gingerly placed my baby in the lap of Jeannette. Noises that only a few could recognize emitted from Jeannette as she squealed her pleasure.

Nina had been a solid and secure person in my shaky and insecure world.

Last year, her Christmas card never came. I went online and tried to find her. I called the last telephone number I had for her. In a world full of lights, glitter and toys, that little cheap card signed with her shaky handwriting meant so much to me. And now she's gone.

For me, it all boils down to the personal touch.

I won't be sending cards out of duty or because someone's feelings may get hurt if they don't receive one. To send a Christmas card is to say to someone important in my life that I am remembering them at this special time of year. And just maybe, this year, I'll take the time for that one handwritten sentence that will give them the personal touch I desire.

It's the Thought That Counts

Typical Christmas shopping has never been on my "to do" list. For years, my plan has been to buy all during the year. If I was in a store for some explicit reason and saw an item that I thought one of my family might like, I would purchase it. Arriving home, it would be labeled and placed on a shelf where it awaited the magic wrapping time. Of course, the process needed to start early in the year for something handmade, like a crocheted or knitted afghan. Christmas gifts have always been on my mind year 'round.

However, that still left me with the wrapping and mailing to do all at once, which was never enjoyable to me. So, at the beginning of this year, I made an announcement to my family. From now on, when I see something I think you might like, I'm mailing it to you at the time of purchase. Think of it as an early Christmas present. I even made up labels that said,

IN KEEPING WITH MY NEW PHILOSOPHY
ABOUT CHRISTMAS, NOW WHEN I SEE
SOMETHING I THINK YOU MIGHT LIKE,
INSTEAD OF PUTTING IT AWAY ON THE
SHELF AND WAITING FOR CHRISTMAS,
I WILL GIVE IT TO YOU NOW.
Merry Early Christmas!!

I face this Christmas with much less stress. I'm crocheting an afghan, which I started in June. Before giving it, I will type a letter to put in with the gift, telling where the afghan has traveled, who I was with as I worked on it, and the prayers that went up for the recipient of the gift.

A few years ago, I received one of my most unique Christmas gifts. It all started when I opened a present and it contained a set of binoculars from my husband.

I NEVER WANTED ANY BINOCULARS!

I thought the gift a bit strange. Stammering out my thank you, I was interrupted by his stream of words regarding these wonderful binoculars. Taking me to the back yard, he spoke of watching the birds in the bird feeder. None of it added up. I laid my hand on his forehead, but he didn't seem to have a fever.

Unbeknownst to me, I had created a dilemma for him. Two daughters and I had planned two Christmas celebrations that year; one in my home and one in another town. My husband somehow missed that memo and thought he was all ready for Christmas (for a change). When the two-part Christmas was explained to him, he panicked and left the house, hurrying to purchase me another gift. The binoculars were "part one" of his gift, which I opened in our home with one daughter and family present on Sunday, December 22nd. Part two was planned for Boise, Idaho with another daughter and family on Christmas Day.

December 25th, I received the second part of the gift from my husband, a pile of website printouts. Each page held the information about a NASCAR racetrack. I was to pick one! WE WERE GOING TO A RACE!!!! You use binoculars at a racetrack. It all made sense. He hadn't lost it after all.

We had a good laugh as he shared with me about the expression on my face when I opened the gift of binoculars and how hard I tried to be nice about them. That's when he explained about the night weeks before, when he had repeatedly gotten out of bed and left the room. Each time, I asked him if he was ok. He always said, "Yes, I'm fine. Now go back to sleep". It had taken him most of the night to print out the websites. Too bad he killed so many trees. I knew before I looked at any pages which race track I wanted to experience.

That was a wonderful present and I enjoyed every minute of the four days we attended the races. I can't say the same for him. As we sat there on the third day, he leaned over and said, "Next year I'm giving you a book".

He actually fell asleep. Next time I go to a race, I'll leave him at home. But as always, it's the thought that counts. He had really good thoughts.

I Have Jesus

The first of the month is always a long day at work for me, so on that August day I worked straight through from 7:30 am to about 4:30. Eager to get home, I was a little dismayed when my husband, John, asked me to leave again as soon as I arrived. He had purchased a new bicycle and very kindly asked me to take him to the cycle shop so he could ride it home.

We pulled out of our driveway just as the 5:00 news came on the radio. We heard the words "two females shot at 26th and S. Edison". When John asked where that was, I felt a wave of concern. "Baxter's" was my answer. Mary and Jack Baxter, and their teenage daughter Jody, were members of a small care group that my husband and I led in our home.

I waited in the car in front of the cycle shop, while John went in to change to cycling clothes and bring his others to me. While he was in there, my cell phone rang. It was a lady from our care group, asking if I had heard about the shootings. Home from work, she had turned on the television. They were showing Baxter's house.

I told John the news update when he came out to the car, and then I headed home. I called the Pastor and he said he would go right out to the house. By now, John was home and he, too, left to go to Baxter's. I stayed home to pray and field phone calls from people in our care group and from the church.

John called to say they were following Jack to the Police Station. John's next phone call was the hardest. He said, "The worst that could happen has happened. They are both gone". Jack had been told his wife and daughter had been shot; murdered in their own home.

It was about 9:30 when John came home. Jack had been transferred to the hospital. John and I stood in the kitchen hugging tightly and crying. We went to bed, but it was a strange night. We lay there awake, every fiber of our beings aching for Jack. John would say something and I would answer. 30 minutes later, I would say something and he would answer. Prayer for Jack was non-stop. How would he make it through?

The next day I called my boss. "I think I need to take the rest of the week off". He understood. I went straight to the church. I didn't know how to contact Jack. He was in hiding from the media. But I knew there would be family to feed. I left the church with an address and phone number. Food would be taken care of until after the funeral.

Our care group met that night. We had a full house. Only Mary and Jack were missing. We had lost one of our family, and we grieved. The pain was very real. But so was the need to do something. The meal planning began. The food would be brought to our house and John and I would deliver it by 5:30 each evening.

The next evening, as we drove toward the address on the piece of paper, we had no idea how to do this. What do you say? His pain would be so much greater than ours.

We carried the food through the house to the kitchen at the back. Jack was on a back deck, saw us in the kitchen and headed in. We met at the door, the three of us in a bear hug, trembling and crying together. No words were necessary. We sat on the deck. The tears were dried. The sky was blue. There was a light breeze. A dog lay at our feet. And Mary and Jody were gone.

Jack began to talk. Of God. Of love. Of peace. Three days after the tragedy, Jack had peace. Peace that could be felt. Peace that could be seen in his eyes. Mary and Jody were in a better place, at the feet of Jesus. And then he said those three little words that I can still hear in my head. Words that instantly changed my perspective. "I have Jesus". That said it all.

That is why that little baby was born.

Christmas is not so we can have more toys and eat large meals. It is not about the decorating and Christmas cards.

It is so we can have Jesus.

Capturing the Spirit

I am very patriotic. I grew up understanding that my older brother served in WWII fighting for our country and had witnessed things he could never speak of. December 7th has always been a day of recognition for me. Most days, (weather permitting) I fly the United States flag proudly from the front of my house.

During my first marriage, I lived in various sections of our United States and was amazed to discover that there were differences among the "united".

When we moved from Oklahoma to North Carolina, we were called Yankees. I always thought Yankees were from the north. The Confederate flag was still flying on many homes and businesses. Since I had very young children, I was still purchasing baby food. Imagine my surprise when Gerber offered red eye gravy and grits in their baby food jars.

In Texas, the town we lived in did not allow "colored" people within the city limits. They would be escorted to the edge of town and asked to leave. Unbelievable!

Growing up in Kansas, I had seen many dust storms. But when I lived in Texas, the dust storms took on a new meaning. Trying to dry my baby's diapers on the clothesline, I learned to keep an eye on the sky and time my washing to coincide with the weather. Sometimes it wasn't the dust, but the black smoke from the refinery in Borger that would cause me to have to re-wash those diapers. The diaper dance would have to be achieved while eluding the ever present flying tumbleweeds.

Maryland was the state that introduced me to draw bridges. We didn't have many of those in Kansas. One day, as my spouse drove us to church, we heard some kind of bell clanging. As he approached the bridge, he did not slow down. The clanging grew louder. I could see a ship in the water below, headed to sail under the bridge. Just as our front wheels reached the bridge, it began to move upward. Slamming on the brakes, we watched as the road in front of us became a hill with a large opening so the ship could sail through.

We weren't in Kansas any more.

I learned about red dirt in Oklahoma. With small children, it seemed that all of their clothes took on a rusty color. They discovered you could do many things with that red dirt; become an Indian with painted face and make designs on the sidewalk (and sometimes the house).

Having lived in Kansas the first 17 years of my life, my world was flat. The first time I was in a car headed west from our town, I thought what I saw in the distance was a row of thunderheads. The closer we came to those clouds, the stranger they looked. I had never seen mountains. After having a glimpse of the Rockies, I wondered why anyone lived in Kansas. I even asked some of the people I knew why they still lived there. Some had never been out of that city; others had never crossed the state border. It was all they knew and they were happy.

Nebraska is where I experienced the goodness of people. That is where I lived when my husband left me, and the church we had attended made it clear I was no longer welcome. Having devoted my entire life in the service of that denomination, I felt abandoned in many ways. Across the street from my house was a Mennonite Church. One day, three women from that church appeared at my front door. They had heard about my troubles (small town) and wanted to let me know I was welcome at their church. How wonderful that felt. Someone wanted me!

Living in Idaho was like living in a totally different country. They didn't have tornadoes. Oh, they said they did, but I had seen real ones. Idaho has mountains and lakes and trees and wonderful weather. I felt like I was living in a picture postcard.

But the one thing I have discovered is that people are people, wherever you live. The color, accent or language does not matter. There are always good ones and bad ones.

I don't agree with everything America stands for. The laziness, greed, and need for instant gratification have caused a meltdown in our economy. But look around. There are many places that are so much worse off than we are. I am grateful that I live in the United States of America.

Blimey…and More

Our first glimpse of what we might be in for occurred at the airport check-in counter in Seattle. Since our seat assignments were in the very last row on the plane, my husband, John, asked if we could get our seats changed. The response given to him, with a very British accent, gave us pause.

"Well, blimey, if you just check with the stewardess, maybe you can get knocked up."

Welcome to another world.

Nine hours later we landed in London, with a train to catch for Edinburgh, Scotland. But first, we hopped on the underground to take us to the train depot. No one had warned me about how quickly they take off. As I was deciding where to sit, we left the station. Suddenly I was on the lap of a lady who glared at me; my backpack in her face. I removed myself to a proper seat, giggling as I went.

At the train station, the board showed a train to Edinburgh on Track 7. We were on our way to Scotland!

Each time the train stopped at a station, the announcement "Mind the gap" was repeated several times. There is a space between the train and the platform. That's the gap. John designed a whole marketing plan for Gap clothes around the saying "Mind the gap".

At Edinburgh, we pulled into Waverly Station and quickly found a taxi. They were lined up in a queue outside the terminal. They looked like they belonged in the 1920's with a queen inside.

We checked in, ate a meal and then walked a block or two looking for bottled water. Little did I know how hard water was going to be to find. All the water is carbonated. We finally found some "still" water.

The next morning, we walked to Edinburgh Castle, an immense complex towering over the city. They named their walls. One was Floddin; another was Telfer. Castles were a town unto themselves. Within the castle walls was every-thing they needed. The cannon fired at 1:00. They always fired at 1:00 instead of 12:00. You see, that way they didn't waste 11 cannon balls.

The United Kingdom seems to care about blind people. Their currency is different sizes for the different denominations. In America, all bills are the same size, from the $1 to the $100. Their question, "How can blind people know what they have?" Good question. So at the castle, when we are waiting in line to go into the vault where the Queen's Jewels are on display, I notice a half wall with models of the crown, staff and rod that we are about to see. These are in metal, with Braille plaques beside them, for the blind people to "see" the Queen's Jewels.

Cars drive on the wrong side of the street.

Lunch time. I now know Scotland has the best baked potatoes in the world. Then we hopped on a tour bus. There was a sign that said "16 passengers - 0 standees". Edinburgh was a very friendly place. People would go out of their way to help you.

One thing I discovered, no matter where I go in the world, I still have to put the new roll of toilet paper on the holder.

The word "blimey" became a regular in our conversation.

We stopped at a little shop. I was looking at a map on the wall. The shop-keeper came up and said "You aren't lost. You are here". In other words, "Why are you looking at a map?"

Instead of saying "yes", they say "aye". A "yield" sign says "Give Way". When lanes merge, it is called an overtake. No parking on the "verge" means no parking on the "shoulder". The word "glen" means "valley". Strath means a big valley. "Brae" means "hill".

Our tour guide took us to Ben Nevis, the tallest mountain in Scotland. He said, "And here you have the highest mountain in Scotland and the lowest hanging cloud". We never saw Ben Nevis.

Everywhere there are clotheslines. People do not use dryers.

There is no time to talk of "Loch Ness" and Braveheart country or Balmoral and Inverness. There are five million people in Scotland. They seem to have a quest for life, not for money.

All too soon, we are home again. But our perspective is different. I cannot be the same person I was. My mind has been stretched, my viewpoints changed. The world is smaller now. I am a better person.

It was wonderful!

A Lovely Neighbor

My first recollection of the word "Canada" came as a child growing up in Kansas. My sister and her family traveled by car to that far-away land and returned with stories of the beauty of Lake Louise and Banff.

Years later, living in Idaho and planning a honeymoon, it seemed only right that we go to Canada. Heading north, we crossed the border and traveled west on Highway 3. Spending the night in a town called Osoyoos, I could only wonder at the origin of that name. As we continued westward, I marveled at the pristine countryside. The town of Surrey caught our attention with its well manicured lawns and an absence of trash lying along the roads.

Stanley Park, in Vancouver, was such a delight. Then traveling north to Horseshoe Bay, we parked at the ferry terminal. Our goal was the ocean side of Vancouver Island. But while we waited for the ferry, we took the time to enjoy some of the best ice cream I've ever had.

Once on the island, we traveled north again, waving to Victoria as we passed. When we reached Highway 4, we cut westward across the island. The streams beside the highway were so clean we could see the rocks on the bottom and the fish swimming. My new husband spied a bear cub, pulled to the side of the road and proceeded to climb out of the car to take a picture. He was given a little lecture on the dangers of a mother close by, but we still have the picture, three cubs in all.

Again, with the strange sounding names for the towns, we came to Ucluelet and then north to Tofino. It was getting late and we needed lodging. Every sign said, "No Vacancy". After a meal and a little prayer for help with finding a spot, my husband's right foot became very heavy as we traveled from one "No Vacancy" to the next.

I placed my hand on his knee and asked, "Do you believe in the prayer we just prayed, asking for help?"

"Of course", was his reply.

"Then why are you going so fast?"

He slowed down to the speed limit.

Finally, we passed a sign where a man was removing the "No". We turned in. They had just had a cancellation. We had a cabin with an ocean view. Beautiful.

My next journey to Canada was not so pleasant. My first grandchild had been born three months too soon in Chilliwack. She was transferred immediately to Shaughnessy Hospital in Vancouver. She remained in that hospital for 117 days. Due to their care, one nurse for every two babies, she is alive today.

Two years later, I returned to Canada again. My trip took me north to Highway 3, turning east to Lethbridge. This time the goal was to retrieve my granddaughter. The Christmas pictures had shown far too many bruises on the child. Other trips to Vancouver have been delightful. My husband and I and some friends spent time there with our visit culminating in a night at "The Phantom of the Opera". It was wonderful!

Through my job, I have made connections with a company in Canada who sold us a software program for my bookkeeping. Every year they hold a "User's Meeting" in Vancouver. I have come to love that city. For a break one evening after all day meetings, my boss asked if I would like to walk around in Stanley Park. Of course, I agreed.

But he hadn't been totally clear about his offer. He meant to walk around the perimeter of the park. When we began the walk, it was a beautiful clear evening. An hour into the walk, it began to get dark and I could see the lights of Vancouver far off in the distance. More walking and we were now on the north side of the park; no city lights. But we were in for a treat. There was an eclipse of the moon and we had ringside seats. Only after our return to the hotel did we discover that it is about seven miles around Stanley Park. Boy did we get our exercise.

One of the best parts about that company in Vancouver is that I have made a new friend. We keep in contact in our off hours too. When my daughter and her foreign exchange student daughter traveled to Vancouver recently, he met them and took them to dinner. He's like extended family.

How rewarding to have nice neighbors.

Bathroom Adventures

Ten years ago, my husband, John, and I took a month-long trip through Europe. In the United States, bathrooms are pretty much the same. Not so over there. I had no idea there were so many ways to flush a toilet. Many times our accommodations did not include a bathtub.

We paid extra for our first tub. It was long, narrow and deep, and we had to go out into the hallway to reach it. Another little tidbit is that all the faucets are individual; either hot or cold. John started my bath for me while I dug for my book to read. I had actually brought a little bottle of bubble bath; just in case I found a tub. I poured some in the water; then reached down to swish it around. Very cold. I pulled the plug and started over. This time we turned on only the hot side, using more precious bubbles.

The tub was hard to get out of. It had a narrow rim on each side and almost no way to push yourself up. Then there was a big step up and over the side to get out. But I managed. John decided to luxuriate too. All was fine until he tried to get out. Through the wall I heard awful noises. Finally, "I can't get out" were the words he yelled. Allowing him time to flounder, I asked (through my laughter) if I could help. Too late. He had made it out.

Since we had both had baths the previous night, the next morning we thought we would just wash our hair. But how to do that with one hot faucet and one cold? John used a glass. He filled it first with hot water and then cold, pouring the glass over his head. I bagged it.

John and I had made a vow to not eat fast food in Europe. However, we really needed to find a toilet, so stopped in a McDonalds for a drink. The stairs to that toilet were down a spiral staircase to a lower floor. Overweight people would have to go elsewhere.

Out shopping for the day with my friend, Diane, while our husbands attended a meeting, we followed the signs to the "toilette". There sat a lady expecting money. I was the only one who had any. I held out my handful of coins, the lady flicked through them, shook her head and motioned for us to go on in.

I had never seen toilets like this before. The seat was recessed in the tank and there was a button on each side of the top of the tank. I pushed one and the toilet flushed. So, I pushed the other. Magically the seat was lowered complete with a paper seat cover. When you flushed, the cover was flushed away and then the seat was again recessed in the tank. Diane and I laughed together afterwards about being trapped until we figured out how to use it. Ladies always flush.

At our next bed and breakfast, the water was cold, which made the shower a small torture chamber. It also took awhile to figure out how to get in. The two sides met at the corner.

Our next accommodation gave us choices. We could have a room with a bed, a room with a bed and toilet, or a room with a bed, toilet and shower. We chose to have it all.

Another room was up two flights of stairs. It was complete with shower and two sinks. The next door down the hall was the toilet. I assumed we were sharing.

The public toilets in Italy were another unique experience. There was an elderly lady sitting in the doorway to collect money. After she was paid her money, the men went to the stalls on the right and the women to the left. The tank was very high on the wall and there was a button in the wall to push for it to flush. The hole in the bowl of the toilet was in the very front of the toilet.

But our accommodations in Florence topped the unusual bathroom arrangements. The bathroom was so small that it was also the shower. The shower head was close to the ceiling across from the toilet. When you were ready to take your shower, you just closed the bathroom door. To relax, you could sit on the toilet.

It's really boring to use the bathrooms in the United States.

Stronghold of Protection

Sitting high above the town, with sheer rock cliffs on three sides, there was only one way into the Edinburgh Castle. When the town was under siege, the castle became a stronghold. The people would gather inside the walls for protection. Within those walls was a self-contained village. Everything they would need was available.

The castle was there for the protection of the kingdom.

We too, have a Kingdom prepared for us, a stronghold of protection. And there is only One Way in. Everything we need is within that Kingdom.

Nicky Cruz grew up on the streets. By age 16, he became a member of the notorious Brooklyn street gang known as the Mau Maus. His life consisted of drugs, alcohol and brutal violence. A friend and fellow gang member was horribly stabbed, beaten and died in his arms. Arrested countless times, Nicky was definitely headed to prison or the electric chair.

One day he met a skinny street preacher named David Wilkerson, who showed him love, relentless love. Enraged, Nicky repeatedly beat him up, spit on him and seriously threatened his life. But David's love remained strong. Finally, having seen the love of Jesus demonstrated, Nicky's walls of resistance were torn down.

Nicky Cruz entered the Kingdom of God.

Mincaye grew up in the jungles of Ecuador. His tribe had many cruel customs. When a man killed another man, the family of the dead man would hunt for the killer and spear him too. Often parents killed their own children, just because they were tired of taking care of them. Mincaye was taught to kill; not only for food but for revenge.

One fateful day in 1956, when he was just a teenager, Mincaye was given a job to do. Those five white men on the banks of the river, the ones he had been eating, sleeping and working with, those men had to be killed.

Joining with some friends, a party of ten Huaorani trekked their way through the trees. Arriving at the river, they began to throw their wooden spears. The white men had guns, but never used them. Their bodies were pierced by the wooden spears of Gikita and Nampa and Kimo and Nimonga and Mincaye and Dyuwi.

Three years later, a sister of one of the white men, Rachel Saint, and a widow of another one, Elisabeth Elliot, traveled to Ecuador to live among the Huaorani. With tender love and much patience, they gained the trust of the Indians. Finally, the day came when the story could be told of why the white men had come and why they had not defended themselves. The Huaorani heard the explanation of why the men wanted to make contact. They came to share about Jesus.

Mincaye and his friends entered the Kingdom of God.

An unnamed Samaritan woman was living a life of sin. She had been married and divorced five times and was now living with another man. She had come to the well to draw water. And then she met Jesus. He loved her; really loved her. She left her water jug and ran to tell others about Him.

Somewhere in this amazing journey, the Samaritan woman who was never named, entered the Kingdom of God. And many other Samaritans from the village entered the Kingdom, because of her testimony.

I grew up in what was designed to look like a castle. We had the high cliffs and a wall around us. But the church I attended built barricades to not only keep the world out, but to keep us in. From the inside, my castle felt more like a dungeon.

But just as all that Nicky knew was how to exist in the street gangs, and Mincaye knew his world in the jungle, I lived as I had been told to, keeping myself separate from the sinners of the world. But the God that loved Nicky, Mincaye and the Samaritan woman, also loved me. He drew me to Him.

And I entered the Kingdom of God.

Being Normal

In my Junior High years, my weight was 140 pounds. Changing into PE clothes in front of all those other "slim" girls was humiliating. It was mandatory that we take a shower after our exercise. Slinking away into a hole would have been preferable.

Since we did not have the money for me to eat lunch at school, by the time I reached Senior High my weight had dropped to 120 pounds. Walking all the way home for lunch had its benefits.

Due to arrangements made by my church, I did not complete my senior year. I married in February and moved to another state. That is when the weight came back with a vengeance. During my first pregnancy, I topped the scales at 154 pounds.

Should I mention that I am only 5' 4" tall?

Not able to lose much weight before the second pregnancy, my numbers went over 160 pounds. Within months I was pregnant again. After that birth, my weight stabilized at 180 pounds.

Several years into the marriage, I became very ill. My digestive system was out of kilter, making me afraid to eat. Eating caused too many ramifications. So the weight dropped off. I finally stopped the downward slide at 106 pounds.

Then my husband left me.

I had no money and a lot of nerves. Macaroni and cheese was cheap. I needed comfort. So I ate. My weight climbed to over 200 pounds.

My sister died at the age of 42, mostly due to overweight. At 5' 2", she weighed around 300 pounds. Her death got my attention.

I began to work on me.

At the same time I was struggling to change my lifestyle, I was scheduled to have a hysterectomy. I listened as the doctor explained that sometimes women gained weight after this surgery, I decided as I sat there that I would rebel against that theory.

You don't gain much weight eating Jell-o. I lost 12 pounds in the hospital. At my first check up, I asked the doctor if I could start exercising. He suggested I walk to the corner and back. That is where I started. As my strength returned, I walked around the block. Then one mile; then two. I gradually built my routine to six or seven miles a day.

I changed my eating habits, eating my last food of the day at 4:00 p.m. With these simple changes, I lost almost 100 pounds over the next two years.

Several years later, I re-married. Now what to do about dinner? It was difficult to cook for someone else and not eat. He really wanted me to sit down and eat with him. I struggled with this issue for several months, even resorting to an appointment with a counselor.

This slim man behind the desk explained to me that I was being highly unreasonable to not sit down and eat dinner with my husband. He carefully detailed how I could eat just a salad or perhaps just a little of everything. I wanted to ask him if he would tell an alcoholic to have just one drink. I was a "foodaholic". But I remained silent.

After a weight gain of 40 pounds, I put my foot down. I needed to stick with what had previously worked for me. So I returned to the practice of not eating after 4:00 p.m.

Over the next year I lost 20 pounds. Then our life became very stressful. We gained custody of our granddaughter. Eating has always been my comfort.

Growing up in a legalistic church, I learned that smoking, drinking, and drugs were sins. But for some reason, overeating was ok.

Before I knew it I was back up to 190 pounds. Once again, I needed to re-gain control of my eating.

My husband had gone on the Atkins diet. No carbs. So I decided to try it. I religiously followed the "carb counting" for two weeks and lost ten pounds. But I could not "stomach" the protein diet (forgive the pun).

I finally integrated all that I had learned about foods into a way of eating that works for me. I am now down to 160 pounds. And I'm still on my way down.

According to the BMI chart, I am only overweight, not obese any longer. Any day now I will reach that magic number that tells me I am "normal". If I stay with my plan, I will become "normal" by the end of June.

I can hardly wait. Do you suppose anyone will notice?

Motorcycles and Blankets

Have you ever been really cold? I mean so cold your legs don't function? I have.

My husband thought it would be fun to ride our motorcycle to the Fiddler's Contest in Weiser, Idaho. It sounded like a plan, and the weather was nice. We put on our jeans, jackets and helmets and headed out, traveling 55 miles down the highway. It was a bit intimidating to ride through downtown Weiser. The main street was lined on both sides with Harley's. We were on a BMW. I didn't have any tattoos.

It was a fun evening. Very late, we decided it was time to head home. Small problem. The temperature was now in the 40's. My husband assured me we would hurry and everything would be alright. He was very wrong.

I became cold. And then I grew even colder. I'm not sure what the wind chill is when the temperature is 40 and you are moving at 70 mph. I was so cold I could not even feel me. I had to assume I was still there.

When we reached home, I could not climb off the bike. I was permanently frozen in the sitting position; feet on the bike's pegs. With a lot of help from my husband, I made my way to a bathtub filled with warm water. I survived. Just barely! I made it perfectly clear I was taking no more rides in the cold.

And so we went to the other extreme.

Have you ever heard of Hell's Canyon? Guess why it's called that.

It was July and we were going to the BMW motorcycle rally in Missoula, Montana. There were about five or six bikes in our group when we left Boise. As we passed through each town, we picked up a few more riders. By afternoon our caravan had arrived in Hell's Canyon.

The sun was beating down on us with the temperature in the 100's. I soon felt like a zombie, with glazed eyes. Concern for my husband flooded me. How could he concentrate on the road? It was all I could do to keep hanging on. Mile after mile went by. Soon a stream wound its way beside the road. How I longed to just lay down in it. But we traveled on. We began to wind our way up White Bird Hill. In the distance we saw a mirage. It said A & W on it. About 50 motorcycles pulled up to have several drinks. Root beer had never tasted so good and so cold!

As we talked, everyone had thought the same thing about pulling over and climbing in the water. But no one did.

The climb up the hill had overheated our motorcycle. When we stopped at a campground for the night, I discovered my clothes had melted to the saddle-bag. I looked lovely with a black hole in the center of my sweatshirt. No more riding in the heat for me.

In other words, I became a fair weather rider.

During another phase of my life, it was clearly demonstrated to me that God certainly has a sense of humor.

When my husband and I first married, he was hot all the time. Even when the temperature was cold out, he would have on shorts and want the heat turned down. I, on the other hand, was cold all the time. When I would ask about turning up the heat, he would respond with, "It's much easier for you to put on more clothes. I can't take anything else off."

And so, I dressed in layers, in my own home, feeling like the kid in the snow-suit in Christmas Story.

But growing older and hormones helped me get my revenge.

He lost a lot of weight. Suddenly he could not get warm. I grew warmer each day. And now we've had a role reversal. I open the windows for the cool breeze and he closes them. I throw off the covers in the night and he grabs for them. He watches television warm and snug under his electric blanket. When the warmth touches me, I shove it away. And when he complains about the temperature of the house and wants to turn the thermostat up, guess what I say?

"It's much easier for you to put on more clothes. I can't take anything else off."

The Cycle of Life

As I worked in the yard, clearing away the debris from the winter, I suddenly discovered a new little shoot pushing its way up through the earth. That new little plant did not care that it had been covered by snow and ice. The dead leaves and dropped flower petals had no bearing on the process taking place under the ground. On my knees in the yard, the cycle of life was clearly visible to me.

As I continued to work, raking away the remnants of the winter, my mind flew back to 1986 when that cycle had been so clearly demonstrated in my own life. In the springtime of that year, I was told I would be having my first grandchild in the fall. I looked forward to the new birth. I love babies.

In July my husband and I moved from Idaho to the state of Washington to begin a new business. His mind was focused on the daily needs of getting a business started. I was seeking employment, temporarily working four part-time jobs to make ends meet. We had been at our new location two weeks, when his

16-year old daughter decided to come live with us. Since we had been "empty nesters" for awhile, we had some adjusting to do.

A few days after her arrival, I received word via my brother that our mother was having difficulty with a sore on her leg. Unbeknownst to us, she had been struggling for months with it. Apparently, she had waited until it was open to the bone before letting anyone know, and she was in a great deal of pain.

She sought medical help. But the situation only worsened.

In August, I received a phone call that my daughter had gone into premature labor. The situation became critical and late that night they performed a C-section, delivering a very tiny little girl. Weighing only two pounds eleven ounces and measuring twelve inches long, Marie began the fight for her life.

She was born on August 5th, one day before my mother's 89th birthday.

Mother's leg developed gangrene.

Marie remained in the neo-natal unit in a hospital in Canada. My mother was hospitalized in Kansas. And my previous place of employment in Idaho requested I come back for the month of October to fill in while my replacement took maternity leave.

My thoughts constantly bounced back and forth between the struggling new life in Canada and the faltering elderly one in Kansas. Such an emotional tug of war. I wanted to be with my husband, with my new granddaughter and be supportive of my mother. Since we needed the income, I remained loyal to my employer.

As October wore on, gradually the reports from Canada became more encouraging and the ones from Kansas were not.

Mother's leg would have to be amputated.

One of my brothers traveled to be at her bedside. She came through the surgery with flying colors. Plans were put in place to release her from the hospital ahead of schedule. And then came the day the doctor spoke with her about going to rehab to learn how to live with only one leg. Apparently, she didn't want to do that. Within the space of 24 hours, she had declined to the point that the doctor told my brother to call his siblings. His words were, "Your mother is shutting herself down. I need to know if you want to put her on life support."

And so the calls were made. We all agreed that if she was shutting herself down, we didn't want to prolong it. At 3:00 a.m. the next morning I awoke with a crystal-clear mind. And I knew she was gone. I received the verifying phone call from my sister at 8:00 a.m.

And so our mother was laid to rest.

Marie's strong spirit had kept her alive and she continued to improve. After 117 days in the hospital, she was discharged to begin her life in the world.

Every day, all over the world, this cycle of life continues. Somewhere, at this moment, someone is dying. And in another place, there is a new birth.

And so I continue to work in my yard. Each day I discard the debris from the winter. And each day I discover another new little shoot pushing up through the ground.

For me, today, I am somewhere between the new birth and the decaying. This is my moment to live.

Concrete and Sponges

I watched the young man's face as we talked. I sensed his emotions had been covered with concrete. He obviously felt the need to remain in control at all times. I listened as Jason's story unfolded. The challenges he had been through. The current trials he was enduring. And through it all, he had analyzed and re-analyzed the issues and arrived at decisions that were best for all involved. Others had not always agreed.

His world was not right and he was going to fix it.

Having talked with many other people in similar circumstances, I knew Jason was not unusual. Humans (may I say especially men) have a tendency to need to be in control of every situation. Any show of emotion would cause a leak in their dike and they might not be able to stop the flow. So they just never let their emotions emerge. They cover them with concrete.

I used to be emotion-less. My feelings were stuffed so far down that I moved through life like a robot. I discovered the physical damage that can do. Stuffing emotions causes all sorts of physical symptoms. Back pain is a common one. I had suffered from colon problems.

Our bodies weren't made to operate with emotions stuffed inside.

As I continued listening to Jason, occasionally I would ask questions. When I asked, "How is that working for you?" he had to admit it wasn't working too well. But he would be strong and conquer.

Later I asked, "Aren't you getting tired of carrying all that baggage around?" I've asked that of others and they always say "yes". But if they lay it down, they have given up control. Too scary! Jason felt the same.

As the days passed, through a mutual friend, I kept in touch with how Jason was doing. The Bible says a "little child shall lead them". Jason's son, William, began going to Sunday School. He got excited about Jesus, and asked Him into his heart. And then William wanted to be baptized.

Jason hadn't been to church for years. He had grown up with legalism and hypocrites. Even though he wanted to be there for his son, he just wasn't sure he could take that walk through the church doors.

William begged.

And so Jason gathered up all the strength he had, got a good grip on his emotions, and entered the church. It was nothing like his childhood church. People were smiling and friendly. The pastor was just a "down to earth" normal human being who spoke in everyday language; language Jason could actually understand.

Then came the moment of baptism. The grin on William's face lit up the room. He had Jesus in his heart and he wanted everyone to know it. A tiny tear leaked out of Jason's eye. That's all it took. The dike broke and the tears flowed. God had spoken to Jason's heart. The concrete began to chip away.

I spoke with Jason a few days ago, and I saw a completely different young man. He has laid down his baggage. His heart is hungry. He wants all his answers today. He is like a sponge, soaking up the goodness of God.

He has plans to be baptized.

The concrete is gone.

Pattern Choices

I stood in the aisle of the store, scanning the various latch hook kits. Having never done latch hook before, I was trying to find an easy one. Making my purchase, I took it home and proceeded to set up my work area. Latch hook uses short strands of yarn of various colors, so I placed each color in a separate baggie. With the pattern laying on the end table beside me and the various baggies of yarn on the floor in front of me, I began my project. Taking one strand of yarn, and using the tool called a latch hook; I poked the hook in and out as I progressed across the first row.

If I followed the pattern, I would end up with a lovely latch hook wall hanging.

Years before, I had tried my hand at cross stitch. Using the same principles, I had a pattern and various colors of thread. The needle went in and out on the piece of cloth where the pattern had been stamped, making an X within each square.

My completed project was a picture of stuffed bears sitting on a ledge; which became a gift for a daughter.

I've been crocheting since I was six. In those days, we didn't have the money to buy patterns, so I was taught to crochet by looking at a completed project. The thread used to make doilies was all one color and very slender. Therefore, the size of the crochet hook had to be very small, to be able to catch that slender thread each time the hook went in and out.

I didn't care for the small thread. It was tedious and took a long time to see any progress.

In my later years, I tired of crocheting, so attended a knitting class. We were given a choice of beginning patterns to try. As I attended class each week, the teacher helped me understand the pattern I had chosen, and the stitch I needed to knit to achieve the desired vest. The knitting needles made a little clicking noise as they went in and out through the strand of yarn.

The completed vest became a gift for a daughter.

But with all these types of projects, they had one thing in common. I made mistakes as I worked on them. Sometimes I could fix the mistake and sometimes I just cut the thread and tried again. A few times I had to unravel and start over. I had a lot of tangled threads on the back of the cross stitch picture.

In one of my knitting projects, I had worked for months on an afghan for a daughter. I was using circular needles; which is one long plastic strand with a needle point on each end. As my needle went in and out, the tension on it suddenly lessened. Not sure what had happened, I laid the partially finished afghan on the floor. In horror, I saw that one of the needle points had come off. I had several inches of knitted loops with nothing holding them in place.

My project was ruined. I certainly didn't know how to fix it. But I remembered the name of my knitting teacher. Hurrying to the phone book, I found her telephone number. When she answered the phone, I poured out my distress to her.

She came right over, bringing a new circular needle for me to borrow. With her expertise, she methodically picked through the loops, restoring my afghan. She refused to take any form of payment, telling me she was glad to help.

The Bible contains many different types of patterns. There are designs in there for Christians, relationships and parenting; to name a few.

In Ephesians 5:21-33, there is a pattern for marriage. God has given us the various colored threads to use. Sometimes it will be tedious and require a lot of give and take. Many couples hop in and out of marriage on a regular basis.

We will have tangled threads and dropped loops. There will be a long span of time before we can begin to see the finished design. There will be times we don't quite understand the project we have chosen, and we need help from our Teacher. In our distress we can turn to the One who already knows what the finished project is to look like, and He has the expertise to restore our marriage.

He will be glad to help.

Invisible Boundaries

I grew up about two blocks from "colored town". There was a distinct, though invisible, line between the "coloreds" and the "whites". I was white. Across town was "Little Mexico". They had their own shopping area and knew they were not to mingle with the "whites".

Somehow the white people were special.

Attending elementary school, I discovered the white people to be snooty and stand-offish. I never connected with them. But with the passing of time and repeated eye contact with one black girl, we cautiously began speaking to each other.

Her name was Linda Hutcherson. She was nice.

She never came to my home and I never entered hers. But we connected at school because we were both the underdog in our worlds. She, because of her color, and I, because of my religion.

Entering Junior High, I lost track of Linda. It became common knowledge that the color to fear was not black, but dark brown. The Mexicans would slice you open if you looked at them wrong. You never, ever wanted to cross the boundary into their town.

Jesse Solis was his name. When I had to pass him in the hall, my heart pounded in my chest. Would he hurt me? Avoiding eye contact, I passed him safely almost every day. But I never knew when it would be my turn to be the brunt of his viciousness.

In my high school years, my future had been designed for me by my church. I was told whom I would marry, therefore; there was no point in making friends of my own. I would belong to Ray.

Ray became friends with a black guy named Randy. He invited us to visit his church for a special service. That is how I ended up in colored town, sitting in a church full of black people.

The music was unbelievable! I had no idea God would allow you to enjoy the songs you sang in church. And they moved their bodies as they sang, yet no lightening bolts struck them. They acted like they knew what they were singing about. Their white teeth shone clearly in their black faces. They had something I did not.

It was difficult to return to my church and sit through the solemn singing of the hymns. I longed to jump up and begin swaying and lifting my hands. Each time that feeling flitted through me, I would pray and ask for forgiveness. I was attending the one true church and we knew how to do it correctly.

Marriage took me to a town in Texas where any person of color would be escorted to the city limits and asked to leave. I always felt conflicted when I heard someone had been driven out of town. How was I better? But I kept my concerns to myself. My opinions were not needed nor wanted.

Years later my husband left me, and I slowly became a different person. I came to the understanding that color didn't matter and that my religion was not the only one going to heaven. I began to see each person as an individual.

In my own personal growth efforts, I joined an organization called Toastmasters. Then came the day I stood before my club to give an Interpretive Reading. I had chosen "God's Trombones". In my childhood I had heard a record of it, being read by James Weldon Johnson, a black man with a very deep and expressive voice. It had resonated within me.

As I began my reading, I could not help but notice my friend, Edgar, sitting right in front of me. His grin stretched from ear to ear. Edgar was a black man with a wonderful deep voice. I am a 5' 4" white woman. I could say the words, but they would never measure up to James Weldon Johnson or Edgar.

After the meeting, Edgar laughed with me as we talked about my puny efforts.

As I think back to Jesse Solis, I wonder what kind of young man he was. Did he know that the whites were afraid of him? Since then, I've worked with Mexicans and found them to be loving and caring people too.

The church I attend today has more whites than any other color. But all are welcome. Recently, as we were listening to the sermon, I heard the wonderful sounds of a deep, black voice saying, "Amen"… "That's right"… "Praise God"… as the pastor spoke.

I'm sure my grin was from ear to ear.

Role Models

Nana was a bitter woman. Others were out to get her. Even her own family wouldn't cooperate with her demands sometimes. She especially didn't care for me.

She was my mother-in-law.

Her childhood had dealt her a bad hand. They had been poor. Her mother was a mousy housewife. She was determined to be different. Her tongue was razor sharp and she directed it at anyone who dared to question what she said.

As a pastor's wife, she had a lot of targets. Around the dinner table after church on Sunday, she spouted non-stop tirades about how the members dressed, how they sang and if they put anything in the offering. Nana felt each little girl should arrive at church with black patent shoes, frilly dresses, hat and gloves. The church members were mostly farmers. Their little girls did farm labor and wore plain, sturdy clothes and shoes.

She couldn't stand it.

So, after raising her two sons, she decided to acquire a daughter to dress as she pleased. It took a lot of court battles and seven long years, but she finally had a daughter. Although she had been named Charlotte, Nana changed her name to Kay.

Each Sunday, Kay had a new frilly dress complete with accessories.

But the bitterness remained. No one complimented Nana on the way Kay looked. So Nana tried harder. As Kay grew older, she became aware that the other children did not like her. She cried on my shoulder many times about not feeling loved at home. Standing in a Christian bookstore one day, I pointed to the plaque on the wall that talked about the love for an adopted child. "You grew in my heart, not under it". Kay had no idea an adopted child was supposed to be loved. She felt like a dress up doll.

I watched this pretentious behavior unfold daily from the time I was twelve until her son left me when I was 29. Nana remained bitter to the end.

Nana's antithesis came in the form of a sweet old lady whom I and my children called Grandma Geller.

She had a hard life. Her husband had died prematurely and her son (and only child) had been severely injured in an accident. His caregiver for years, she never complained, but always had a smile. When he died, she grieved and then moved on.

It was her idea to call her Grandma, since we had no grandmas. For us, Grandma Geller was a rock in our unstable world. We were welcome at her home any time. If it was close to a mealtime, she opened her heart and kitchen to us. As we sat at her table, we could watch the hummingbirds as they feasted on the feeders just outside the window.

Her yard was a profusion of flowers, and she always sent me home with a bouquet. When I married again, I drove to her house the morning of my wedding and she provided the flowers for my special day, including the ones I wore in my hair.

I could turn to her for advice on any subject.

One day, when my children were with their father, I mustered up my courage and drove the 22 miles from Nampa to Boise to sit by the river. The spot I chose just happened to be on the grounds of the Red Lion Motel. Sitting on a bench, minding my own business and pondering life; suddenly an older man dressed in a suit appeared and sat down beside me.

I had no idea what to do. Should I run? Scream? Be nice? This was one of my first ventures into the world. Did this kind of thing happen often?

We talked for awhile. He seemed nice. As he stood to leave, without any warning, he turned and kissed me full on the mouth as he pressed a $50 bill into my hand. He walked away, while I wondered what kind of germs had just been transferred to me. And what was I supposed to do with this $50? I felt dirty.

I went straight to Grandma Geller.

She gave me wonderful advice. "Honey, the devil has had that money long enough. You go out and buy yourself something new. Consider it a gift from God."

I did.

Now You See It, Now You Don't

I sat on the floor of the gymnasium with the other kindergarten children. Our Christmas program was in progress. The air was buzzing with excitement. When the program was over, we would be dismissed for our Christmas vacation. For most of the kids, that meant Christmas parties and lots of presents under a tree.

We had a tree. It was about eight inches tall and made of clear plastic. I wasn't too excited about it. It was supposed to have a gum drop on the end of each of the branches. We didn't have any gum drops. I would attend no parties. There might be one gift for me for Christmas.

Final remarks were being made when the speaker was interrupted with a hearty "ho-ho-ho". Santa had arrived, with a bag slung over his shoulder. Who knew what was in there?

He started with the youngest children. That was my group. As he reached into the bag, he withdrew a brown paper sack and handed it to a child. Repeatedly, his hand disappeared into the bag and re-appeared with another sack. All around me, the shrieks of the others added to the excitement. They ripped their sacks open and discovered they were full of candy.

It was my turn. I politely reached for my sack and said, "Thank you". And then I sat back down and just waited to be dismissed. I knew I was not allowed to open the sack until I got home. Candy was a rare experience in our family and I needed permission before I ate any.

Soon we were dismissed. Children were shouting and running everywhere. I quietly pulled on my boots and winter coat. I had several blocks to walk. And the snow was deep out there. Tucking my paper sack under my armpit, I headed west into the wind that contained spits of new snow.

As I trudged through the snow, I thought about the candy in my possession. Would mother let me eat any? What kind was in there? Would I like it? Maybe I should save it for Christmas Day. That way, if I didn't get anything for Christmas, I would still have candy.

I slowly made my way home. My arms were full of my books and papers, making the going tough. Finally, I reached West Street and turned north. Just a short distance left to go. I climbed the steps to our front door. Laying my books and papers down so I could reach for the doorknob, I felt under my arm for my paper sack.

Something was wrong. It felt weird. As I pulled it out where I could see it, I discovered an empty sack. Apparently, the movement of my arm back and forth as I worked my way through the snow had rubbed a hole in the sack.

Like Hansel and Gretel, I had left a trail behind me; not of crumbs, but pieces of candy. I felt no sense of loss. It was still unclear to me if I would have been allowed to eat it. And I was still unsure if I would have liked it. I had no real experience with candy.

I threw the empty sack in the trash and began to take off my boots.

The Waiting Place

I sat by her bed and held her hand. Her name was Anna and her body was the shell she lived in. Paralyzed by a stroke, her eyes were the only part of her body that contained a spark of life. Now she was dying. I worked as a Nurse's Aide in a nursing home. In the twelve months I had worked there, no one had ever visited Anna.

My shock and dismay over the treatment of the patients who resided there had been almost overwhelming. What mattered was the money. It seemed no one saw these people as human beings. There were the few who sat day after day in front of the nurse's station. Strapped into adult highchairs, they drooled, babbled and banged on their tray all day.

Vivian was a resident who had the air of southern aristocracy. As I changed the sheets on her bed, she remained aloof from my small conversation. It was very clear I was the hired help. Then came the day she needed some repair on her bathroom door. The handyman, named Clarence, had black skin. When

Clarence entered Vivian's room and walked toward the chair where she was sitting, she stood as she reached for her cane and began to beat him on the head.

Someone else would have to fix that door.

Harry lived in a world of torment. As I carried out my duties in his room, he delivered a stream of vile words directed at me. I had never heard most of those words before. But with the hatred in his voice, I knew they weren't nice ones.

Helen's room was an oasis of calm. She always greeted me with a smile and sometimes an offer of a cookie. Her gratitude for a newly made bed washed over me. I felt appreciated and needed.

And so came the day when my shift was over. As I headed for the door to leave, I overheard the conversation at the nurse's station about Anna. Plans were already being made for the new patient who would occupy that room. The new patient's family had been called. It was only a matter of time.

Immediately I made a U-turn, catching the attention of the nursing supervisor.

"Where are you going?" she asked.

"To be with Anna" was my simple reply.

"Oh, that's not part of your job. You can go on home" she said brusquely.

"I don't want her to die alone", I said softly. "I will sit with her."

"Just make sure you clock out first. We won't pay you for staying" was her terse answer.

Anna heard me enter. Her eyes locked with mine. She knew.

I sat down and took her lifeless hand in mine. I leaned close to her face and said, "Anna, I know you can hear me. I just want you to know I will be here with you".

A tear leaked out of her eye and ran toward her ear. I wiped it away.

"Anna, do you know Jesus? Blink twice if the answer is yes".

Instantly she closed her eyes and opened them twice.

"Then soon you will be free of this body and be running and jumping down the streets of gold. Are you ready for that?"

Two blinks, and more tears down the cheeks. Once again I wiped them away gently. I had never done this before. A part of me wanted to leave the room and forget it was happening.

But I could not leave her alone.

I sang softly and prayed and kept my eyes locked on hers. When they closed, I felt a catch in my breath. But the rise and fall of her chest told me not yet.

It didn't take long. She was ready. Anna gently slipped away.

I sat there in silence. I conjured up a mental image of Anna, whole again. I had been a witness to a wonderful passing. Selfishly I hoped I would never end up like Anna; an active mind trapped in a lifeless body. I prayed I would remember this moment of Anna's release.

Still holding her hand, my reverie was interrupted by the strident voice of the nursing supervisor. "Why didn't you tell us she died? We need to get this room stripped and disinfected. The new patient is arriving at 8:00."

I was ushered from the room as the flurry of activity began. I wondered what they planned to do with Anna's body. But I knew Anna no longer cared. She was free.

Imitating the Cheshire Cat

Months before my 65th birthday in December, I gave my husband, John, a warning. I planned to buy a car I wanted. Not one that got me from here to there. Not one purchased for the gas mileage. For my 65th, I was going to splurge. I wanted a car that would make me grin.

One of our friends, Ken, sells cars. One day as we all sat around at Starbucks, John informed him I was going to buy a car. And the questions began. "What kind? What color? What price?" But I poked a hole in Ken's bubble.

"I'm not ready to buy yet. Give me a few months to get some bills paid off and then I'll start looking in the fall" I told him.

He heard me.

The next time John began discussing the kind of car I wanted, Ken gave me a smile as he told him, "I'll wait until she says she is ready".

Ken had me right where he wanted me.

A few months before my intended goal of beginning my search, I happened by Ken's dealership to get an idea of what was available. I wandered through the cars. I test drove one. It didn't make me grin. I tried another. No grinning.

But Ken had listened to me when I said what I wanted. He ushered me to a car and said, "I think this one is what you are looking for."

I grinned as I drove away from the lot. More grinning as I returned.

The first of June is our anniversary. John and I were going out to dinner that evening. Ken suggested I test drive the car to the restaurant to meet him. It was a few more months before I planned to buy. I was just looking. I have never liked shopping and truly am not an impulse buyer. But there was all that grinning.

To make our anniversary special, John had plans to go away that weekend with a motorcycle group. As he held my hand at dinner, he mentioned all the grinning.

"Why don't you call Ken and tell him to start the paperwork?"

My husband left town for the weekend and I bought a car. I opened the windows and the roof. I turned the XM radio to a jazz station. I drove south into Oregon. I drove north, back through our town and past the city limits. It grew dark. But I couldn't just go home. I drove to Starbucks and sat with the yuppies. I don't even drink coffee. But that car sure looked good in the parking lot. The grin seemed permanent.

I needed to drive more than just a few hours. So, plans were put in motion for me to take a road trip. With a daughter in Pasadena, CA and one in Salem, OR we looked for a central place to meet. Clear Lake, CA was the chosen spot.

On a beautiful, clear June morning I headed out with a "non-stop" grin. Turning south at Biggs Junction in Oregon, I transitioned from freeway to two-lane highway. I had been on this road before. It is winding, tree-lined, and hilly. That makes it very difficult to pass the big logging trucks. I traveled behind a truck for miles. Finally, I could see a straight stretch of road ahead. As I pulled out to pass, I pressed on the accelerator. There was no struggling to get by. As I flew by the truck, I exclaimed out loud to myself, "Oh, wow. I could get used to this".

Passing was no problem anymore. More grinning.

The miles flew by. The sky was blue. Mt. Shasta was beautiful. The summer weather totally cooperated as I continued my solo journey. 700 miles later, I arrived at my destination. As I showed my new purchase to my daughters, I was still grinning.

After a week and another 700 miles, I returned home.

Just as my husband loves to hop on the motorcycle and take a ride, I truly enjoy getting behind the steering wheel and taking little drives of 200 or 300 miles. When I used to ride behind John on the bike, he would tell me, "Just be one with the bike". I've discovered I like it much better to be "one with my car". I plan to put that theory to the test a lot through the long summer days.

When the snow flies, I can pull out my memories and grin again.

Life in the Blender

We had become a "blended" family, and I use that term loosely. I had three daughters and he had one. In the nine years I had been single, I had taught my daughters to become self-sufficient; doing their own cooking, laundry and managing their own money and to think for themselves.

His daughter was a little younger and had been taught very differently. He was used to her behavior. The blending wasn't going too well. It was going to take a lot of adjusting.

One day he came home after a long day at work. Two of my teenage daughters were sitting at the kitchen table doing their homework. As he walked through the kitchen to the bedroom to change his clothes, he sat a paper sack containing two hamburgers on the corner of the table. It was to be his snack.

When he returned to the kitchen, he could not find his hamburgers.

I heard his sputtering and hurried to the kitchen. Practically doubled over in laughter, I tried to explain about the concept of not sitting food in front of teenagers and then leaving the room.

He didn't think it was funny.

We made some new rules. No more sitting food that you planned to eat in front of teenagers. And for the teenagers, ask first.

So Lyn did ask. When he came home with a watermelon, she asked, "Is that for me?"

As he slid the watermelon into the refrigerator, he answered, "Sure".

Later that evening, Lyn went to band practice. He headed to the refrigerator for a slice of watermelon. It was gone.

Life was certainly frustrating.

Lyn had a fun time at practice and came bouncing through the door on her return. He met her with a question. "Did you do something with my watermelon?"

Her response, "I asked you and you said it was for me. I took it to band practice and shared with everyone".

He had meant she could have some. She had taken him literally, that it was for her.

More discussion.

One of the things I had learned as I made my way through the land mines of being a single parent was never react to what they said. Reactions stop all communication. So when I re-married, that was one of the concepts I shared with my new husband.

Just listen.

One day, as we drove Lyn home from school, he demonstrated to me that he had learned that lesson very well.

From the back seat, Lyn asked, "How do you know if you are pregnant?"

His hands may have tightened the grip on the steering wheel, but he hit no telephone poles, nor did he run over any curbs or people.

I calmly began explaining the changes in the body and symptoms that might appear if you were pregnant.

"Ok," she said. "Lori (her friend) thinks she might be and was afraid to ask her mom. I told her I could ask you."

Once again, all was well.

My two youngest daughters were in marching band. It was Lyn's last year in high school and René's first year. Lyn really wanted me to chaperone the band as they went out of town to a competition. René didn't want anyone to know I was her mother.

I sat in the back of one bus with Lyn and her friends. René rode in a different bus. When we arrived at the stadium, René stayed as far away from me as she could. Lyn and her friends accepted me as one of them and we were having fun.

Suddenly, René appeared at my elbow.

"Mom, I need to talk to you", she said.

"I'm sorry. Do I know you?" was my response.

"Moooooom, I really need to talk to you".

I decided to be her mom again. Together we averted what she considered a catastrophe. When the crisis was over, she returned to her bus, once more avoiding me.

Then there was the time René lost someone else's baby. She had gone to babysit. A little later, she came home, frantic.

"Mom, I don't know where Julia is. I took her down to the school to meet with some friends. Mary took her to show to someone else. And now I can't find Mary or Julia".

So much for a relaxing evening.

But all is well that ends well. By the time we returned to the school, Mary had returned. Julia was fine, and René had some new rules to live by.

Living with teenagers is about learning to live life in the state of flux.

Tornado Alley

They call it "tornado alley" for a reason. In the spring, cooler air flows over the Rockies and collides with warmer air flowing up from the Gulf. When these two systems collide; watch out.

I grew up in "tornado alley".

My mother and I lived in two upstairs rooms. The only way down was via an outside stairway. Mother would wait until the storm was blowing down trees and lightening was splitting the air before she would yell run. The chase was on as we headed for a neighbor's basement. I always wondered why we couldn't go there a little sooner.

One time my sister, her husband, my brother, my fiancé and I went to a race in Topeka, Kansas. Home was about 90 miles to the southeast down the turnpike. My fiancé, brother and I were in one car headed home. There were lightening strikes all around us and the wind was buffeting the car from side to side.

Then the car began to sputter like it was going to stop running. We managed to get under an overpass before it totally died. Along came a highway patrolman.

"There are tornadoes all around this area", he said. "If you see one coming, climb right up there", and he pointed to the area where the ground met the overpass. We were to lie down and cover our heads.

The car shook as the wind blew. Hail was pounding on the front windshield, and my heart was pounding in my chest. Suddenly there was an instant calm. Then the assault came from the back side of the car. Something had passed over us.

My brother and fiancé wanted to stay with the car, but they flagged down a motorist and asked if I could hitch a ride to the nearest toll booth. I mentally voted "no" to that idea, but the car door came open and I was ushered into the car of strangers.

Would I ever see my family again?

I'm not really sure that being left in a toll booth on the turnpike was exactly a wonderfully safe place for me to be. But I did have a ringside seat for the lightening and funnel clouds. A few minutes later my sister and her husband came along. My brother had flagged them down and told them to stop and pick me up.

My fiancé and I were married the next February. We moved from Kansas to Oklahoma. It was Easter time and we were going home for our first visit. It was a beautiful spring afternoon when we left Bethany, Oklahoma. As I had sewn my own Easter dress, I needed to get the hem in it before I could wear it.

Head down, intent on my sewing, I never saw the wall of clouds that we had driven into until it suddenly turned dark. Looking up, I could tell we were going to be in trouble. The clouds were ripe for a tornado.

Just after we crossed the state line from Oklahoma into Kansas, I watched a funnel begin to form a little to the left of the turnpike. As it moved across the ground, I could see trees being uprooted and objects flying through the air.

"Please turn around", I said meekly. I NEVER told him what to do.

"You can't turn around on a turnpike", was his reply. He kept driving straight for the funnel.

I asked again. Same answer. But up ahead we could see the lights of cars that were dipping down into the median and heading back the way we had come, trying to outrun the funnel.

We turned around.

The first building we came to was a little restaurant aptly named The Failing Café. It would not be much protection, as it truly appeared to be failing. Since we had skipped supper to get on the road, my fiancé ordered a hamburger. Just as his food was placed in front of him, the electricity went out. He ate in the dark.

Many people who lived in "tornado alley" had some kind of a radio that didn't need electricity and would still give you the tornado warnings. Sitting in the dark, I listened as we were told the funnel was gaining in size and speed and headed for us. It passed a little to the east and we survived. When the all clear was given, we climbed in the car and headed north again. Side note: he forgot to pay for the hamburger.

I love the springtime living miles away from "tornado alley".

Who Moved

God was gone. When I prayed, it felt like I was talking to myself. I had heard the phrase "winter of the soul". I was in the Arctic.

I knew how to pray. I could use good words like "Thee" and "Thou". I understood how to use repetition and quote scriptures as I prayed. These things I had been taught before I could speak. Now my words bounced back.

Where was God?

My husband had left me. I had no job, no skills and no money. I had three children and a body full of terror. Having been raised to do the right things, I just kept on doing. But it wasn't helping.

Day after day, the freeze continued. I read my Bible. The words were just words, without meaning. Since my husband had left me, our church told me I was no longer welcome. So, I had no fellowship, no Bible study to attend, and no friends.

I was turning to ice.

One day I stood in my kitchen and looked toward the ceiling. Yelling at God had never been in my repertoire, but I had reached the end. I heard my mouth questioning God.

"What are you doing? Where is all that strength you promised? I can't take much more. I need answers."

I waited for the lightening bolt. I still lived.

Not knowing anything else to try, I continued to read my Bible and pray. I became a robot. Day after day passed. Still no God anywhere.

As the weeks went by, I began to just talk to God as I worked around the house. I knew it wasn't being reverent and I wasn't kneeling, but I needed someone to talk to. After I survived several sessions of talking, my initial fear that He would do something to me for being so disrespectful dissipated.

He really was gone.

So I stopped reading the Bible. No more praying. I spent that time inside my head, checking myself out. What exactly did I believe? Why did I believe it? Was that belief in the Bible, or was it just my mother talking? Did I want to be like my mother? I was afraid to be honest with myself. God wouldn't like it.

But something was very wrong.

What kind of parent could I be when I was so numb? How could I answer their questions when I had no answers for my own?

The ice was about to crack and swallow me up.

There had been no tears. Deep inside, I knew I deserved whatever punishment I was receiving. Therefore, I accepted that this was how my life would be. No feelings. No warmth. Just frigid existence.

But my religious training kicked in. Not reading the Bible and not praying made me feel even worse. So I tried it one more time. Lying on my stomach across the bed, the Bible open beside me, I prayed one last desperate prayer.

"God, I need you to help me. Please show me what I'm supposed to do."

Would you believe that the Bible just happened to be open to Jeremiah 29:11? Those are the words my eyes fell on, when I lowered them to read.

"For I know the plans I have for you," declares the LORD, "plans to prosper you and not to harm you, plans to give you hope and a future."

Obviously I had not understood the words correctly. The God I knew did not care about prospering me or giving me hope. His job was to make sure I toed the mark and did everything right.

So I read them again. Yep, they still said the same thing. I read them again and again. The words stayed the same. But deep inside me I felt a tiny spark of warmth. I had been taught the Bible was true. So could I believe these words? Why had I never heard of them before?

In my despair, I longed for something to hang on to. I continued to read those words. The warmth spread. I talked to God again. It began to feel good. Did He really want to give me hope? Where had He been?

Gently I heard Him say, "I'm not the one who moved."

Slowly, ever so slowly, the ice began to melt. I began a relationship with a friend; one I could talk to.

He had been there all the time.

Inadequate Instructions

The child was hungry…no…starving. But the medical professionals were unaware of that. He had two parents and a nice home. Nothing to suspect there. The doctors could not find any illness causing the downward slide in weight. If it continued, the baby would have to be hospitalized. And then who knew what would come next.

They lived in another town, but I heard of the baby's plight. I was very busy sewing dresses for my daughter's wedding. But the thought persisted.

"Go and observe. See what's happening at home."

I loaded my portable sewing machine and my husband into the car. Praying as we headed down the highway, I asked God for guidance and wisdom; to help me see what He saw.

Placing my sewing machine on their kitchen table, I talked with the young parents as I worked on the blue satin.

The baby was crying. It was time for a bottle. The young mother walked past me into the kitchen. Reaching into the cupboard, she retrieved a two-ounce baby bottle. Pouring some formula powder in, she then put in the warm water and shook the bottle. Returning to the living room, she handed the bottle to her husband, who began feeding the baby.

Within minutes the little bottle was empty.

As the daddy removed the nipple from the baby's mouth, the infant began to scream and thrash around. Placing the baby on his shoulder, the daddy rose from the couch and began walking around, bouncing and shushing the child.

"Why is that all you gave him to drink?" I asked from my chair at the table.

"Oh, that's all he is supposed to have", the mother replied.

"He's still hungry."

"Well, this is what we were told to give him", she responded.

I'm sure the concern showed in my voice. "Well, that's not enough for him to drink. Make him another bottle. Don't you have any bigger than that?"

"No, this is the only size we've ever had. He's only supposed to have two ounces at a time. That's what they told us when we left the hospital."

Rather intensely I said, "That was six months ago. He needs a bigger bottle now".

The daddy said, "If we feed him more, he'll just throw it up. I'll get him to sleep in a minute. He wears himself out and falls asleep. But he never sleeps very long."

I was through discussing.

Grabbing my purse, I said to the mother, "Come with me. We are going to buy some eight-ounce bottles. You are going to fill it with formula and let that baby suck until he is full."

She didn't argue.

Upon our return, an eight-ounce bottle was prepared. Under my direction, I made them continue feeding the child (with burping occasionally) until he fell asleep with the nipple in his mouth.

"Now, that's what is supposed to happen", I told them.

When the baby continued to sleep past his usual 30 minutes waking time, the mother began to get worried. "Should I wake him up? He's never slept this long before."

"Apparently, he's never had a full tummy before. He is sleeping contentedly. He will let you know when he's hungry again", was my sage advice.

I had discovered the cause of the downward slide in weight. My job here was done.

The Schism in my World

Would tonight be the night? Had I been good enough? I knew I had placed my books softly on the table and completed my homework. I had ironed 12 shirts (mother took in ironings for a living). What more did I need to do? Just maybe I would get to go to Joan's and watch a program on T.V.

Would it be "I Love Lucy"? She sure was crazy, stomping those grapes with her feet. Or maybe it would be Spring Byington in "December Bride". Some nights it was a mind stretching program called "Twilight Zone". There was always a twist at the end. During those 30 minutes I would be busily trying to come up with the conclusion. I guess my thoughts just weren't bizarre enough. I never did get it right.

But best of all was the night that the black and white, tiny screen in the corner would show a line profile and then Alfred Hitchcock would walk onto the screen and fit his face into that profile. I knew we were in for a treat. Throughout the whole program my brain was buzzing, trying to stay a step ahead of the plot. On a really good night, I figured it out before the end.

In preparation for the television viewing, Joan would place a quilt on the concrete slab floor of the little living room. Ann, Sara, and I would get our pillows and get ready for our entertainment. Since "Eata Bita Popcorn" was a business that was run out of the back room, we usually had popcorn to stuff in our mouths.

Some evenings, we just gathered around the piano, pulling music from a cardboard box containing sheet music. We sang until our throats gave out; songs like "Coming In On a Wing and a Prayer", "Stardust" and my favorite, "Sentimental Journey".

Joan also played an accordion. It was fascinating to watch the back and forth movement of the instrument, while at the same time she moved both hands on different kinds of keyboards to play the song. One side looked like a piano. The other side had round buttons to push. She needed a three-sided brain to make music.

Since playing with regular cards would be a sin, we made up games with the Flinch cards. Joan had pointed fingernails, so you never wanted to sit across from her when you played Slap. She was serious about winning, and you could get hurt if you got in her way.

At bedtime, we all headed for the standard-size bed, so it was a wee bit crowded when we piled in. Scary stories would be told, complete with sound effects. One night, the scary story happened outside the bedroom window. It was summertime and the windows were open. The closest house was across a vacant lot. The slamming of doors caught our attention. Our eyes grew wide and our hands reached for each other as we watched two men carry a body out of the house and place it in the back seat of a car. Without turning on the lights, the car backed out of the driveway and drove away.

Boy, did the stories fly then. Was the body dead? Where had they taken it? Should we call the police? Sleep eluded us that night.

Joan cooked the very best fried chicken and her roasts were so tender they fell apart. Even though I would be stuffed to the gills, I would finish off the meal with a piece of her delicious Dutch apple pie.

All too soon, my stay at Joan's would be over. She would drive me across town, I would climb the outside stairway to the two rooms where I lived with my mother, and my life would revert to its former environment. I felt like I had been on a 24-hour pass and had now returned to my prison. The warden always met me at the door.

We had no T.V. The radio played non-stop sermons. My meals consisted of oatmeal for breakfast; no raisins or brown sugar. Lunch was a hamburger patty, no bun. Boiled potatoes and green beans from a can would complete the meal. We drank room temperature water. Cold drinks were bad for you.

I honestly don't remember eating dinner.

Bedtime meant I had to sleep with my mother. Hanging off the side of the bed so I wouldn't accidentally touch her, I would long to return to Joan's. She made my childhood so very special.

She was my sister.

A Three-Letter Word

As a child, I could look from my upstairs window and watch the neighborhood kids playing in the yards and street below. I had such pity for them. They probably didn't even know they were going to hell.

As I grew older and walked down the halls of my Junior and Senior High Schools, I was careful to avoid any contact with the sinners. Attending school functions with them was strictly forbidden. The scripture said to "come out from among them and be ye separate". I had that one down pat.

In church twice on Sunday and once in the middle of the week, I mingled with adults who knew they were going to heaven. After all, only members of our denomination would make it there.

Proverbs 16:5: "The Lord despises pride; be assured that the proud will be punished."

Pride is a sin. Ow!

My church made it clear that drinking, smoking, and drugs were sins. Sitting in the pew, watching a 300-pound preacher declare that "your body is the temple of God and it is up to you to take care of it", I wondered (in fear and trembling) if there wasn't something wrong with being that heavy.

My life was not pleasant. And I had been taught by my church and family that to crave food for comfort was ok. At 5' 4", weighing over 200 pounds was certainly not taking care of my temple. But at least it wasn't a sin.

Or was it?

1 Peter 4:3: "You have had enough in the past of the evil things that godless people enjoy…feasting".

Gluttony is a sin. Ow!

As a young married couple, we made friends with another young couple. As we got to know them, we discovered many things about their life; when they married, when their four children were born. I pondered the information and realized that they had not gotten married quite soon enough for that first child.

Sitting around a dinner table one evening, the names of that young couple came up. I didn't point out the error of their ways; I just stated when they got married and when their first child was born.

A few days later I received a very tearful phone call from the young lady. She no longer wished to be my friend. And why had I felt the need to share that she had to get married?

Proverbs 10:18: "….to slander is to be a fool".

Gossip is a sin. Ow!

Sin; persistent, habitual doing of wrong.

Who Knew

As a NASCAR fan, I couldn't help but notice the sponsor's advertising on the cars that we stared at for hours. Some sponsors were very familiar. Others I had never heard of. One in particular caught my eye. Alan Kulwicki was driving a car with a huge owl on the hood. Smaller owls decorated the sides of the car. The eyes of the owls were also used for the "O" in the word "Hooters". I'd never heard of Hooters, but knew they were a sponsor of some kind; apparently something to do with owls.

My husband and I attended a business meeting in Tempe, Arizona. We had been traveling all day; arriving at our destination tired and hungry. In the lobby of the hotel, we met up with several of our business peers who had also just arrived. As we exited the front door, the conversation centered on finding a place to eat. Imagine my surprise when I spied a name I recognized on the side of a building right across the street.

Hooters.

Very excitedly I suggested we eat at Hooters. Now I knew what kind of sponsor they were and I had an opportunity to eat at their restaurant. I noticed some strange looks from my friends, but they all agreed that would be the place to eat.

The restaurant was upstairs, with a large deck. As we crossed the deck headed for the front door, a very scantily clad young lady greeted us. I've got an open mind, so I adjusted to the lack of clothing and we were ushered to a table.

Looking around the room, I discovered that ALL of the waitresses were dressed that way, and they ALL had something in common. My friends were looking at me instead of their menus. Some began to snicker.

What was their problem?

My waitress bent low to take my order. My eyes were level with her cleavage. Suddenly I understood what the word hooters meant. I wanted the floor to swallow me up. I remember exactly the grain of the wood, because I studied it for the next few minutes. I don't know what I ordered. My peers laughed so loudly others turned to see what was going on. The heat from my cheeks warmed the room.

Who knew that's what it meant?

We attend that meeting in Tempe annually. Each year, when it's time to decide where to eat, someone always announces, "I know where Joy wants to eat. Hooters."

I may never live it down.

Motorcycle Moments

I should have seen it coming, when my husband asked oh so innocently, "Instead of our usual Friday night date, could we go look at motorcycles?" Huh? Motorcycles? Why hadn't I thought of that?

24 hours later we were the proud owners of a 1997 Honda Shadow Spirit with 1,100 ccs. I was sorry I asked about that last part. I really didn't want to know 1,100 ccs meant it had a lot of power and could go fast.

Saturday evening we had our first motorcycle discussion when he thought my car should now reside outside the garage to make room for the motorcycle in the garage. Huh? Boy was he wrong.

5:15 Sunday morning, and my husband was getting up.

"John, are you OK?

"I'm too excited to sleep. I'm going for a ride."

And so, good little wife that I am, I got up to see him off. Right? Wrong. He had told me what he was going to do, and I wanted to watch and possibly laugh.

We had ordered helmets, but they hadn't come in yet. So, he was going to have to use a helmet that was over 20 years old. The inside was all torn up and little black flakes were coming off. To keep the black stuff from getting all over his balding head, he placed a washcloth on his head before he put the helmet on. You gotta love him.

The helmets still hadn't arrived by Wednesday and he just couldn't wait any longer. He wheeled the motorcycle out of the garage; we got on and sat in the driveway in front of God and all the neighbors, while he gave me instructions.

"Just be one with the bike." He held up his hand and pointed to the palm. "This is the bike". As he pointed to his thumb, he said "This is you. The bike leans this way," he said as he leaned his palm over, "you lean with it. It leans the other way; you lean the other way."

Huh?

Then he decided we needed some signals to communicate on the road. He held school right there in the driveway.

He stood behind me and patted me on my sides. "This means OK or yes". Pushing with his hands from side to side on my waist he explained that would tell him I planned to adjust my position. He ran his hands up my sides, explaining that would mean "I don't know what you said". As he rubbed his hand back and forth on my back, he told me that would mean "no". Rubbing up and down on my back I was instructed that would mean "Stop the next chance you get". Poking one finger in my back he indicated that would mean "Stop now!"

Huh?

The helmets arrived on Thursday, so we discussed taking a short trip. A four-hour ride to northern Idaho was not my idea of a short trip. But that weekend we headed out. Right away I noticed he was giving me a signal we hadn't talked about. He was holding his left hand out and pointing to the side. Huh? A few miles later he did it again. What was he trying to tell me? Was he pointing to roadkill? Then I noticed that he only did it when we were meeting a motorcycle going the other way.

It was a motorcycle wave.

Since I had been straddling the bike for over two hours, I decided it would be really nice if I could just put my legs together. I rubbed up and down on his back. He got to a stopping place, took off his helmet, looked at me and said, "I don't know what that signal meant". Huh? They were his signals.

After a break, we headed on north. An hour later, he pulled into the driveway of some friends, turned the bike off, put down the kick stand and suddenly his foot was headed my way. He was getting off! I said what any typical female would say. YIKE!

He turned and stared at me. His eyes said, "Who are you and what are you doing on my bike?" He had forgotten I was back there.

I held up my hand, pointed to my thumb and said, "I was just being one with the bike".

I'm sure we will have many more experiences with this new purchase. How about black leathers with fringe, and possibly a tattoo or two? Huh?

Road Rage

I have a lot of people fooled. They think I am a calm, level-headed senior citizen. They have never seen me behind a steering wheel in a car that is moving down the road.

Are the other drivers incapable of reading the speed limit signs? Do they not understand that to turn right, you really should be in the right lane? Don't get me started on the teeny bopper who is chewing gum, talking on the cell phone and smoking a cigarette.

I try to be very aware of the speed limits (since I have a propensity to go too fast). But when the sign says 35, I would like to go faster than 20. I follow the slow poke for blocks. It's a side street with one lane each way. Finally I can take it no longer. Glancing in my rear view mirror, I pull to the left and floorboard it. In no time, I'm around and going the speed limit…35. I leave them in my dust.

Our town has roundabouts. It seems I always have the pleasure of being behind the driver who does not understand how to navigate them. The most common offense is when they pull up to the roundabout and stop. No cars are coming from any direction. Apparently stopping just seems like the thing to do. I honk. They set and wait until a car enters the roundabout. Then they decide it's their turn to go, following the lead of some kind of secret internal clock that only special people possess.

How about the ones who think the left lane of the freeway is for the slow cars? I watch as car after car goes around on the right side. Then it's my turn. Just about the time I move to the right, they get it. They, too, move to the right. I can never let down my guard. They are everywhere.

I realize that signals on the car are a very new invention. Most drivers are not yet aware they can actually move a little lever by the steering wheel and it tells folks in the other cars that you are planning to turn. Some drivers have figured out that lever is for signaling a turn, but they haven't yet mastered the fact that blinking the left turn light means that is actually the direction you plan to turn.

I especially enjoy sitting at a stoplight, my car vibrating to the beat of the stereo in the car next to me. I can feel the bass pulsing in my chest with my heart beat. Many times the words are nasty. I feel totally invaded.

A few years ago, I was driving down a street that has two lanes going each way. I was in the left lane, planning to turn left. I had no cars behind me. I pulled to a complete stop, waiting for a hole in the traffic going the other way. I kept glancing in my rear view mirror. As I waited, my blinker signaling my planned turn, my foot on the brake, I saw a large white car in my rear-view mirror coming toward me in my lane. Glancing at the oncoming traffic, I still saw no way I could turn left. The white car loomed larger and larger. God made a hole in that oncoming traffic just as the white car slammed into me. My car was knocked clear through the other lane and against the curb.

A young man jumped from the white car, ran to my passenger window (which was down), poked his head in, and said, "I was just planning to go around you."

What would you say to that?

Then he explained that we really didn't need to call the police. He would just give me his insurance information. I was busily assessing whether I was ok. But by then a few other people had gathered and they prevented him from getting in his car and driving away. They called the police.

He didn't have any insurance.

And to add insult to injury, when they fixed my car, they had to totally replace the back end, which meant I lost my back bumper, which had a Dale Earnhardt sticker on it. The auto mechanic pronounced, "You are going to have to lose Dale Earnhardt."

My husband tells me I can't drive anywhere right after watching a NASCAR race. I'm pumped and just waiting for the chance to do a "bump and run".

The Long Slide

Hidden away in the Bavarian Mountains are salt mines. Some very well-meaning friends urged my husband, John, and I to visit a mine when in Austria. I believed their glowing reports about what a wonderful time we would have on a tour.

Arriving at one of the mines, the first thing we had to do was put on white scrubs over our clothes, to keep our clothes clean. This was not a good sign. Just what had we gotten ourselves in to? We all (and that means all the strangers standing there in their white scrubs) were instructed to straddle a metal bench sitting on a rail. I didn't know who was in front of me; but I grabbed a hold of them. John climbed on behind me. We traveled on this bench into the mine, leaving the daylight behind. After climbing off, we walked further and further into the mountain, through old mining tunnels.

Soon we arrived at a wooden contraption. When its function was explained to us; I voted "no" on the rest of the tour. It was two highly polished wooden rails side by side slanted downward. Two at a time, we were to straddle these rails and slide down to the next level. It was so dark down there we couldn't see the bottom. But there was no way to go back. John sat in front of me while I clung to him with all my might, needing him to protect me from the danger. Down we went; sliding so fast our thighs burned.

Phew! I was still alive at the bottom.

Through more tunnels, and we kept going. I spied another slide. Everything within me said "I don't want to". Our guide informed us this one was three times longer than the first one. In fear for my life, I climbed on. This time John sat behind me to hold on to me and give me comfort. (It didn't work.) We slid down….and down…and just when I'm wondering when this will end, a flash goes off in my face and they've taken my picture. Swell! I'm sure they used it in some dictionary to describe the feelings of terror.

We ended up 650 feet below the surface of the mountain; and lived to tell about it. Phew again!

Do you remember, as a child, climbing to the top of the slide in the park? Were you afraid to let go and begin what seemed like a very long slide to the bottom? Maybe Mom was standing there to catch you. How safe did you feel when you trusted her and just let go?

I've been on some other slides in my life. Standing at the top and looking into the deep, dark hole, I voted "no" on taking it. But life does not work that way. Some slides come with the word cancer. Other slides might be called divorce. If you've lived very many years, you've been at the top of some of life's slides.

As a Christian, we have some wonderful promises about Someone who doesn't wait at the bottom to catch us, but climbs on the slide and goes down the slope with us. He wraps His arms around us and holds us tight.

The Message puts it this way in Psalms 91:4: "His huge outstretched arms protect you…." Or Psalms 63:8: "…your strong right hand holds me securely."

We don't have to go on our scary slides alone. We have a Friend who will be right there with us; even when it is that last big long slide of death. At the bottom we will reach the beautiful place He has gone to prepare for us where we will live eternally.

Phew! What a relief.

Secrets

SECRET #1

Ilistened as the young lady told me her story. Attending college miles from home, she had gotten pregnant. In her embarrassment, she had told no one, determined to go through the nine months alone. Since abortion was not an option, she made plans for adoption.

With her pregnancy in full bloom, she met a very nice young man. As their relationship grew, she finally opened up to him and told the whole story. He vowed to be by her side through the coming days.

He was her labor coach. Then he helped her through the first days after she gave the baby up. When life had settled down, he declared his love and asked her to marry him.

As she talked, her youngest child played at her feet. Her three other children were in various parts of the house.

"No one but my husband knows of the other child" she told me.

But now I did.

SECRET #2

The young lady sat on the couch, fidgeting with the sleeves of her coat. The room was warm enough for the coat to be removed. But she had a secret she needed to keep covered.

"I don't know how to make it through some days. I feel like my body has betrayed me."

I listened as she told her story. It seemed the only thing that mattered to her was the size of her breasts, or lack of. She had what is called "Body Dysmorphic Disorder".

In the preliminary phone call from her, before our meeting, I had realized how very serious this issue was to her. So, I had done some research and discovered the disorder and that it can be so severe some sufferers commit suicide.

Body Dysmorphic Disorder is defined as an excessive preoccupation with an imagined or a minor defect of a localized facial feature or body part. People with this disorder view themselves as ugly or misshapen.

Even though she had the tall, lean body of a model, she was embarrassed about who she was. The smile she wore on her face was a cover up for her very low self-esteem. She led a busy life, attended church, and chauffeured her children to their various school and sports activities. But she always wore a loose-fitting top or jacket. She didn't want anyone to know her secret.

But now I did.

SECRET #3

The young man had such a serious look on his face. He was sharing about the young lady he had fallen in love with, and about the secret he was keeping from her.

"She is a nice Christian lady and she doesn't know I ever smoked."

As the conversation continued, he shared more and more of his past with me. Drinking. Drugs. His children aborted. And he was worried she would find out that he had been a smoker?

He lived in another city. It seemed unlikely that I would ever meet his wife, but if I did, I was to share nothing of his words today. It seemed he just needed to download all his secrets so he could have a fresh start. His love would never know of these issues in his past.

But now I did.

~~~

SECRET #4

I knew the middle-aged lady sitting across from me. We attended the same church. Something was really bothering her. Soon we left the surface talk and her distress poured out.

A few days before, her husband had gone off to work as usual. Even though she rarely called him at work, she needed to ask him a question that day. She was very surprised to be told he had taken a vacation day. That evening he arrived home just a little later than normal. She confronted him with her discovery; but was not prepared for his answer when she asked where he had been.

"I spent the day at a nudist colony."

She agreed with him, when he said no one else should ever know.

But now I did.
~~~

Words in a Book

When I was struggling through the de-programming of my religious training, I stumbled across a book called "Your Erroneous Zones" by Dr. Wayne Dyer. Upon completion of the book, I immediately read it again and again. The thoughts in that book were totally contrary to the beliefs of my church.

Yet, thanks to that book, I learned I did not have to live daily with worry and guilt. I wore the original book out, but have a copy on my bookshelf today. The words in that book were an inspiration to me that helped change my life.

In a book entitled "Beyond Ourselves" Catherine Marshall wrote a chapter on "The Prayer of Relinquishment". I had been taught to pray telling God what I desired, such as healing, and then He was obligated to do what I asked. When you pray the prayer of relinquishment, you are, in essence, telling God that you are willing to let Him decide what is best for you.

Another life-changing concept. The inspiration I received from those words has helped me many times in my life. I have a copy of that book on my shelf.

The title of the book was what caught my eye. Jess Lair, Ph.D. authored a book called "I ain't well – but I sure am better". It was inspiring to discover that each day I could be better than I was the day before. I still have a copy of that book on my shelf.

Rosalind Rinker wrote a book describing prayer as a conversation with God. As I began reading it, my fear of the heresy within its pages almost prevented me from progressing through the book. I knew "prayerese" – using King James language and praying to impress others. The concept of just talking to God seemed disrespectful.

The inspiration I received from the words in that book changed my prayer life forever. It, too, has a special place on my bookshelf.

These books that hold so much meaning for me were written in the 1960's and 1970's. Yet they are still so very special to me today – in the year 2019. How satisfying it must be for authors to realize that their words on the page helped trigger personal growth in someone's life.

As a writer, I pray that some day, some where, some how, I will write some words that inspire someone to change their life for the better; words they will carry with them throughout their life.

Choices

I felt like a kid in a candy store. I had an afternoon in a motel room all to myself. Hours to spend. What would I do first? Read? Write? Crochet? Take a walk? Do my nails?

It was my choice.

My mind flashed back to my childhood. Stott's Grocery had been situated on the alley at the next intersection from where I lived. Bins of candy. And sometimes I would be lucky enough to have a penny to spend. How was I supposed to choose only one piece of candy from the vast array displayed there? Who knew when I would get a penny again?

But I could choose.

That's what it feels like to walk into a bookstore. It contains so much more than bins of candy. One aisle is full of hope for those who feel hopeless. The next aisle contains books that help you study the Bible. Depending on the size of the store, there may be several floors of choices.

Powell's Bookstore in Portland, Oregon is just such a place. My daughter took me there once. It took hours to pull a book from the shelf, read a little and then replace it; over and over again. So many books. Not enough time to read all of them, and not enough money to buy all of them.

How could I choose?

With the advent of video games and Kindles, will the children of today ever know the magic of walking into a bookstore?

The Art of Listening

Listening is more than just hearing words. Those words need to register and take on meaning. A basic human need is to understand and be understood. Good listening skills will help in that process.

Apparently Jesus knew that you could hear the words, but not really listen.

In Matthew 11:15 – He said, "Are you listening to me? Really listening?"

Mark 4:9 – "Are you listening to this? Really listening?"

Mark 4:23 – "Are you listening to this? Really listening?"

It seemed important to Him that we really listen.

Every day, all day, our ears are bombarded with sounds. Most of the time we don't even hear them.

Did you know that the birds in your back yard can give you information? They will tell you when they are happy, when they are mad, and even when a cat has entered the yard. Have you ever heard the birds in your yard?

Or maybe it's the television you've never really listened to. Do you hear the words coming out of that box? Listen with different ears this next week. You just might be surprised.

Maybe it's your children or grandchildren that you just really don't listen to. Are you busy reading the paper or watching television when they are trying to tell you something that is important to them? See if you can hear what really matters to them.

Here is a little "Listening Test". Carefully read ALL parts of following test before doing anything.

1. Write today's date (month, day, and year) in the top right hand corner of a piece of paper.
2. Write the answer to the following multiplication problem directly underneath the date on your paper: 6 x 5 = ?
3. In the lower right hand corner of your paper, draw a rectangle.
4. Directly above your answer to #3, draw a row of three small circles.
5. Hold your right hand up in the air for three seconds.
6. Scratch your head.
7. Now that you have carefully read all parts of the test, don't do anything but sit quietly.

Do you remember what my instructions were? "Carefully read ALL parts of the test before doing anything".

How well do you think you listen? I did not ask "How well do you hear?"

Hearing is not the same as listening. Hearing is merely one step in the process. Listening involves receiving, organizing, interpreting, and responding to the information that is heard. Sometimes we need to listen with our heart.

When you are truly listening, then you are willing to try and understand the other person's point of view. That shows genuine respect for the opinions of others. Active listening reduces certain kinds of communication breakdowns, stimulates communication, promotes positive feelings of self-worth and helps people better understand each other.

A person who likes to listen acts like a good listener. They focus their eyes on the person who is doing the talking. They are attentive and lean forward, responding with facial expressions to show they are enjoying what they are hearing.

In Psalms 116:1-2, it says: "He bends down and listens". That means GOD LEANS FORWARD TO LISTEN TO US!!!! That is a sign of a good listener.

In every communication, there is a sender and a receiver. The problem is too many people are sending and too few are receiving.

Psalm 116:1-2 in the "Message" Bible says, "God listens INTENTLY as we pour out our hearts to Him."

Should we do any less for others?

Taste of Freedom

The eagle's egg didn't belong in the prairie chicken's nest. It was an experiment. The mother hen did her duty, sitting on the eggs and keeping them warm. Finally the time came for her little babies to peck their way out. They learned to scratch in the dirt and eat the grain scattered on the ground.

One day the baby eagle heard a new sound and looked up into the big blue sky. He had never seen an eagle soar before. He fluttered his little wings and moved a few feet low to the ground.

"What must it be like to soar; free and high?"

But he was a prairie chicken. He lived the rest of his life scratching in the dirt and eating grain scattered on the ground, never leaving the pen, never knowing he was an eagle.

I grew up in a religious atmosphere, full of rules and "should nots". Guilt and worry were my daily companions. To be carefree and laughing meant you weren't serious about God. Occasionally I would catch a glimpse of life outside my pen; just a taste of freedom.

"What must it be like to be free?"

But I was a Christian. I was destined to live my life with my head down, being pious for God.

Life happened. I married and had children. My husband was a preacher. My pen was very small with very high walls and certainly no freedom. I wasn't allowed to look up and see any blue sky.

I never thought to myself, "What must it be like to soar free of bondage?"

When my husband left us, I lived my life by rote. I knew the rules. God was watching. I couldn't look outside the pen. There would be no taste of freedom for me.

Then came the day my brother came to my door. His words painted the picture of my life; scratching in the dirt and eating the grain from the ground. He wondered if I ever looked up. My eyes remained steadfastly down. I belonged here.

He didn't give up. He drew pictures of a different kind of life, one that included a taste of freedom. I could soar free. He didn't understand. Freedom was for the non-Christian. God would strike me with lightening if I looked up into the big blue sky and even thought of wanting out of my pen.

My brother persevered.

Slowly, oh so slowly, my chin came up. Were his words a possibility for me? Eye contact was made. His smile told me he believed every word he was saying. But he was explaining a life to me that I had never tasted. Hours later I finally uttered the words he had been waiting for. I was willing to try my wings, fly over the wall, and get a taste of that freedom he had been sharing about.

My wings were weak, having never used them. Life outside the pen was scary … and wonderful.

When it finally registered, deep down inside, that what God wanted for me was an abundant life, I became absolutely giddy. My co-workers accused me of having a secret boyfriend.

I had never known I was an eagle.

I've discovered talents that lay buried all those years. Humor surrounds me every day. Each morning is a gift. My guilt and worry have been thrown away. And as I soar with my eagle's eye. I look down and see the scratching in the dirt and eating of the grain on the ground by the people who still function as prairie chickens because they have never yet been told they are eagles.

My heart goes out to them. I long for them to taste the freedom I've found.

"The thief comes only to steal and kill and destroy; I came that they may have life and have it abundantly." (NASB John 10:10b)

Change of Address

Come with me to the dark, wind-swept land of my childhood. In that barren place, it was decreed that all Christians must be devoid of emotions. My church and my widowed mother were in agreement. To have feelings was to sin. My mother never touched me nor told me she loved me.

We lived in two rooms upstairs. From our window, I watched the neighborhood children in the yard below. My distance from them kept me safe from their sin as they laughed and played. Even at a young age, I understood I was to never dance around, yell and roll on the ground.

I moved through my days detached emotionally from life.

One day, as a teen, I came home from school and placed my books on the table with a thud. Instantly, Mother's strident voice came from the other room. She said, "Lois, shame on you for being so upset. Get your emotions under control. On Sunday you can go to the altar and ask for forgiveness for what you just did."

I didn't argue or question. I knew the drill. Even though I hadn't been upset, on Sunday I would be escorted to the altar at the front of the church, surrounded by other members of the congregation, to pray for my forgiveness.

I remained stoic when Mother told me whom I would be marrying and when. I was only 15 when plans were put in motion for my marriage before the completion of my senior year in high school. Just as I had no reaction to being led to the altar to repent of my sins, I registered no feelings as I walked down that same aisle during my wedding ceremony.

Pledging to love, honor and obey the man standing at the end of that aisle was no different than being told to love, honor and obey my mother. In either case, I was to do as I was told.

But deep under the crust of my obedience lurked a feeling…of love. When I held my firstborn, I struggled to put a cap on the emotion that came bubbling up from within me. It was now my job to be a role model for this little one, teaching her to keep all emotions under control, lest she sin.

Trying to teach a child to have no emotion is as effective as trying to nail Jell-o to the wall. With three daughters in five years, it was an impossible task. And I had feelings, conflicted feelings, about stifling their happiness. I reached deep into a reservoir I didn't know was in me when I allowed my oldest to dance, yes, dance, in our living room, even though her dad was ordering me to make her stop.

Life went on. Their dad left. I took two years to decide on the kind of mom I desired to be. One change I would make would be the removal of the ban on emotions. I seated my children on the couch and stood facing them. They stared at me wide-eyed as I made my declaration.

I said, "From now on I am going to be different. You will be hugged and kissed by me. Daily, I will tell you I love you. We will laugh and have fun. I will help you become who you were meant to be."

The transition time was difficult. I worked at erasing old programming while I reached out to hug them. I would place my arms around them and feel their bodies become rigid in response. The act of touching was new to all of us, but they worked at accepting my efforts. Hugs that had been stiff and duty driven became warm and loving. The "I love you's" sounded regularly as they headed out the door and again before bedtime.

Feelings were now welcome in our home.

The barren land is a distant memory. My life is sun drenched with gentle breezes and flowers, as hugs occur spontaneously. As we have gotten older, we don't kiss as much when we get together. But the love comes through with hugs, smiles and laughter. I love you's are placed at the end of communications by text, email and phone calls.

There is an added bonus in this beautiful land.

I have a husband who loves me, sits and talks with me, holds my hand as we walk and hugs me daily.

Title: Conversations with Myself

My hand gropes through the darkness, searching for the origin of the noise that has pulled me from my dreams. I squelch the alarm and fumble for my glasses. Lost in the mist of waking, I wonder what day it is. Oh yes, it's Tuesday. So that means I have a hair appointment at 4:30. My feet touch the floor. Sliding them forward, I insert my feet into my house shoes.

Is this the day for the house payment? No, I think I still have two days before that's due. Feeling my way through the dark bedroom, I reach the bathroom door, enter, and close the door behind me before I turn on the light. I hope I didn't wake him up.

I mustn't forget to put the drops in my eyes. Guess this is something I will do the rest of my life. But there are others who are so much worse off. I'm thankful the medicine is working. Opening the drawer, I take the top off the eye drops bottle as I raise it to my eyes. I can't hold my eyes open wide enough for the drops without opening my mouth. Wonder why that is?

Putting on my exercise clothes, my mind wanders to the podcasts I been listening to by Chuck Swindoll. Will he still be talking about the renewing of the mind today? And I mustn't forget to put on my baseball cap. Don't want to scare anyone at the gym. As I tie my tennis shoes, I review what Chuck said yesterday. I remember what it was like to feel renewed. How wonderful it is that I am not the same person I used to be. I am so very blessed.

Grabbing a jacket, I turn out the bathroom light and grope my way across the bedroom to the door. Once I'm in the kitchen, with the bedroom door shut behind me, I turn on the kitchen light. So far so good.

Should I check my email before I go exercise? I head down the hall to my office. After a few deletions and one reply, I'm ready to go. *God, please be with Christy as she goes through this trial.* Grabbing a bottle of water out of the refrigerator, I wonder if I have any food to take to work for lunch today. Should I go by the store on my way home from exercise?

Is it time for the news? I climb in the car and push the button to turn on the radio as I back out of the garage. How awful for all those people who can't catch fish for their income anymore. Will BP take care of them? Or will it end up like Katrina? Did I remember to shut the garage door?

Not many cars at the gym. Is this a holiday? No, it's just a Tuesday. Guess they decided to sleep in. So, what am I doing up at 4:30? Because I don't want to end up like Joan. She died way too young.

On the treadmill, I place the headset on my ears. I don't want to make eye contact. They will want to talk, and I really need to hear what Chuck Swindoll has to say. Do I have time to do two miles this morning? I can if I don't go to the store on the way home from here. Guess I'll just have to make do with what I can find in the refrigerator. I really need the two miles.

Satisfied with the exercise I've achieved; I change from listening to the podcast to music. What do people do that don't get pleasure from music? How can they stand it? Instantly I'm off on a mental journey of all the beloved music I know, and so I hum and sing my way home.

His car is gone. Guess he's already at Starbucks. After I clean up, I'll just make the bed and straighten up so I can go to work early. That way I can leave early in time for my hair appointment.

Fast forward. Workday completed, hair appointment over, I stop by the mailbox on the way home. How in the world have all these catalog companies found my new address already? They sure kill a lot of trees. Good. No bills this time.

So goes the day. Constant dialogue in my head.

Masks of Many Designs

The school bus reverberated with the sound of teenage voices excited over their win at the choir competition. Don, their director and bus driver, smiled as he heard their comments. He rounded the curve and headed west through the darkness on the two-lane highway. Home was an hour away.

Patchy fog floated over the road. "Could you please talk a little softer?" Don asked. "I need to concentrate on my driving."

Halfway home the unbelievable happened. The headlights on the bus went out. Don frantically tried to find the side of the highway while he pushed the brake pedal. Suddenly he was facing the headlights of an oncoming truck. There was a grinding crash as bus and truck collided.

Through the screaming and moaning, Don's voice could barely be heard. "How badly are you hurt? Talk to me." The noises subsided as each student reported in. No one was seriously hurt, no one but Don.

In a calm voice, he requested, "Would you do something for me? Please sing It Is Well with My Soul." The kids kneeling close to Don understood this was not just a simple request. Don was dying.

Word trickled to the back of the bus. His students crowded around him. The singing began. Through the darkness, the sound of teenage voices rose, voices quavering, as they performed one last time for their teacher.

Before the paramedics arrived, Don had gone home. He hadn't planned to go there tonight. But he was ready for the trip. Don's inner person witnessed to his students that he had peace in his final journey.

Gail was the typical jolly, fat soul. Happiness just oozed from her pores. Even though she was short, she stood out in a crowd. She was the sounding board for young people who always gathered around her.

Very few people knew that one morning, after her husband and children had gone for the day; she blew out the pilot light in the oven, turned it on and stuck her head in. Her plan might have worked, except her husband forgot something and returned unexpectedly.

Only those of us who were the very closest understood the turmoil she dealt with every day. Looking like the Pillsbury dough boy created a deep sense of shame and worthlessness.

Her inner person just wanted to die.

When Anna sang, her audience was captivated by the sound of her voice as it rolled over them. A picture of poise, she stood straight and tall, energizing the room with the feelings evoked by her song. Applause was long and loud.

Anna dressed like a model with every hair in place. She exuded an aura of money and upper class up-bringing. But even in the warmer weather, she always wore long sleeves. In conversations about her, the story was passed along that she was always cold.

Anna was a "cutter". To help herself feel alive, she needed the pain and the blood. She lived alone and no one knew her inner person was in torment.

He was black, unemployed and couldn't speak good English, and he lived under a bridge. Most of the time he had no way to bathe, so didn't smell very good. But Custer had pride and didn't want any handouts. If you were willing to give him a meal, then he would do some work in return.

When you saw Custer, the focal point was his smile stretching from ear to ear; all that white in his black face. Custer had Jesus. His inner person saw way beyond this life and looked ahead to heaven.

My Gift to You

Mother, in my journey toward wholeness, I have come to understand that I need to forgive you. Over the past months, so many memories have flooded my mind; pictures of the childhood you stole from me. The teen years I never had a chance to enjoy. A marriage of my choosing with someone I loved.

Today, I sit with a group of people my age and they reminisce about the music of the 60's. They smile at me and say, "I'm sure you remember when Elvis sang, " and they name a song I've never heard of. They didn't know that kind of music was a sin. Or they talk about the prom they attended, the clothes they wore and the romantic evening they enjoyed. Dancing was also on the list of sins. It was a little worse than tapping my toe in time to any music that might slip through on the radio.

Here's what I remember about my childhood. Me sitting in the window watching the neighborhood kids playing in the street. Since they didn't go to our church, they were obviously going to hell and I could not associate with them. I listened to my classmates at school talking about the current movies. I could not go to a movie. They were of the devil and the roof of the movie theatre might fall on me. Television was the devil's box and only evil came out of it.

I loved to roller skate. When I turned 10, you explained I could no longer enjoy that. Because of my age, it was now a form of dancing. Playing cards was strictly off limits. Any game that contained dice was a sin. I never quite understood what was wrong with dominoes. Swimming was called "mixed bathing" in the little black book that we lived by. The church's manual outlined each and every sin in detail.

And so, you listened to sermons on the radio … KJRG … Newton, Kansas. And I sat quietly in the corner, trying very hard not to sin.

Where would I have learned anything about real life? My religious cage kept me from the world and things of the world; which meant anything and everyone that did not agree with your religious beliefs.

And then there is the marriage issue. I remember your announcement to me at the age of 15 that before I finished high school, I would be marrying the preacher's son. You were right. I did. I had only thought I had a hard life when I lived at home. Thirteen years later, when he left me, you asked, "What did you do to him to make him leave?"

And so, what do I do with all these memories? And what about the ones I never got to have? How do I just say, "Oh, that's ok?"

Now you are in your 80's. Do I really think you are going to change? Understand? No.

The last time I attended church with you I was a woman in my 40's. We sat on the second row (in your pew; it has your name on it) and you reached over to my arm and slid your hand up under my sleeve toward my shoulder.

"Mother, what are you doing?"

"I'm just making sure you have a bra on."

How do I reason with that?

So, I have decided not to try. I believe that if I brought all this up it would only hurt you. I don't believe I could ever make you understand what it was like for me. You might stop all communication. And in your eyes, I would have only sinned again.

I write this letter, intending to never mail it. Even though it has taken months, I can tell you that I forgive you. I can never get those days back and I sure don't want to taint the days I have left with bitterness over my loss.

I really don't feel love for you. I can say you have qualities I respect. You are a strong woman, which I inherited from you. I have always tried to honor you; my mother.

As I continue on my journey to wholeness, I will look back on my life and remember this letter. I can move forward with peace, knowing that my gift of forgiveness to you was to withhold sending you this letter.

Your daughter,

Lois

Dan and Ernie

Their names were Dan and Ernie. I had never known a lady named Ernie, but it seemed to suit her. Angela was their little baby's name. They had just begun attending our church. As the preacher's wife, I attended all ladies functions. That is where I met Ernie.

Usual questions were asked. Where are you from? How long have you lived here? Then somehow the topic of when and where they were married came up. Looking at Angela and hearing the date of the wedding, my mind said, "Oops." But the conversation moved on. Maybe I was the only one who heard it.

Days later, the ladies of the church had a luncheon. Of course, I was there. But Angela was sick, so Ernie could not attend. Since she was new to our group, she became the topic of conversation. I related what I knew of the answers to … where are you from? How long have you lived here? Then came the question about how long they had been married. It was a sin to lie.

So, I just stated facts. Anyone who could do elementary math would know the wedding date was not soon enough for Angela's age. In my mind, I was just answering the questions. No one gasped or threatened to kick Ernie out of our church. When the conversation moved on to other topics, I totally forgot Ernie and her wedding date.

Two nights later the parsonage phone rang. A tearful woman's voice on the other end of the line said, "How could you? And why did you? It wasn't anyone's business." Ernie had been confronted about the wedding date. Was that the real date or had Lois made a mistake? I was Lois.

Now what should I do? It didn't make any difference to me when Ernie was married.

"Ernie, I was just stating facts. I didn't mean anything by it."

"Are you really that naïve? Do you not know that the whole church is now talking about us? Why did you feel the need to let everyone know that we had to get married?"

But I hadn't felt that need.

The phone call did not end well. Ernie was still crying, and I was upset beyond belief. I was so careful to never hurt anyone. And now look at what I had done with a careless slip of my tongue. She had called me naïve. What did that mean?

I looked it up in the dictionary. It didn't seem like a compliment to me.

1. Lacking worldly experience and understanding
2. Characterized by a lack of sophistication and critical judgment
3. Ignorantly simple
4. Sometimes foolish, simple, childlike

It was a hard lesson to learn, but I learned it well. My words had badly hurt another human being. I didn't ever want to do that again. Even if to me I was just stating facts, those facts might become harmful when heard by the wrong ears.

Dan and Ernie did not leave our church, but they avoided me. I followed their progress over the years as they had three more children and then felt called to be Wycliffe Bible translators. They took their four young children and traveled to a jungle to help spread the word of God there.

The natives didn't care when their wedding date was.

Roadside Reading

Mother and I used our feet for transportation; through choking dust storms and freezing blizzards. Mother never graduated to owning an automobile. So, when my sister and her husband offered to take me on vacation with them from Kansas to Wyoming, I could hardly wait. The floor space between the back seat and the front seat was filled with boxes, making a level area for me and my two nieces. Since the car had no air conditioning and it was July, we left at night with the three of us sleeping soundly in our traveling bedroom.

During the day, the billboards and signs gave us plenty of letters and numbers with which to play games. The alphabet game consisted of finding each letter of the alphabet, starting with A, on the signs we passed. The first one to letter Z was the winner. Unless you were passing by a zoo, a Z was hard to find.

But my very favorite discovery was the Burma-Shave signs. They were every-where … and such fun to read. A little bit of trivia. The first recorded signs were put up in 1927. By 1930 the company had 19 different sets of phrases.

In 1938, safety messages were added … such as:

Don't take a curve
At 60 per
We hate to lose
A customer
Burma-Shave

Hardly a driver
Is now alive
Who passed
On hills
At 75
Burma-Shave

Past
Schoolhouses
Take it slow
Let the little
Shavers grow
Burma-Shave

If you dislike
Big traffic fines
Slow down
Till you
Can read these signs
Burma-Shave

It's best for
One who hits
The bottle
To let another
Use the throttle
Burma-Shave

Some slogans added a little humor:

Don't stick
Your elbow
Out so far
It might go home
In another car
Burma-Shave

Don't lose
Your head
To gain a minute
You need your head
Your brains are in it
Burma-Shave

If you
Don't know
Whose signs
These are
You can't have
Driven very far

And then they left off their product name

The company decided to try a special promotional message:

Free offer! Free offer!
Rip a fender off your car
Mail it in
For a half-pound jar
Burma-Shave

They received a large number of fenders and made good on their promise.

I'm sure the trio in the back of the car made the ones in the front seats miserable. We memorized the slogans and repeated them again and again. Even though 60 years have passed, I can still remember the anticipation of waiting for the next sign to appear.

Outsider in Our Midst

He stood in the doorway to my singles' class, unsure of what to do next. Welcoming him, I motioned to a chair. His name was Scott and he had never been to church before. But he was lonely and thought maybe he could find some friends in my class. I read between all those lines. Did he already have his eye on one of the young ladies?

As the members of the class filed in, I introduced Scott, with handshakes all around.

The lesson that day was on Shadrach, Meshach and Abednego. Discussion was lively, as various ones spoke of having courage to stand up for what they believed. It was then I noticed Scott's face. He had no idea who Shadrach, Meshach and Abednego were. Therefore, to him, we were speaking a foreign language. Who was King Nebuchadnezzar? Why was he mad at those people? I could just hear the questions in Scott's head.

Raising my hand for silence, I paused before speaking.

"Scott is new to church. He has never heard this story before. Would someone like to explain to him what we are discussing?"

It was difficult to break it down to the bare facts. Everyone in that room, everyone but Scott, had heard the story many times. I persevered, requesting again and again that the story be broken down even more. I understood this information needed to be dispensed as a child's story.

After class, I walked with Scott to the hallway.

"Did you understand what that story was all about?"

Embarrassed, he blushed as he apologized for never hearing it before. Not wanting him to feel ashamed, we talked until I felt he was doing better. I asked if we could meet some other time away from the church to talk again.

We made an appointment.

Week after week, Scott sat in our adult class as we told children's stories to him. The class finally understood he couldn't comprehend our church language.

In our private discussions, Scott would ask questions like, "What does it mean to eat His body and drink His blood? That sounds like a ritual a cult would do." I agreed. It did sound very unusual.

So many words needed to be explained. Redemption. Salvation. Baptized. Crucified. Foot of the cross. What did these words have to do with religion? What was the difference between religion and being a Christian? The questions went on and on.

I asked Scott if it was okay for me to purchase him some books from the Christian bookstore, books designed for children, explaining our beliefs. We took one book at a time, one story at a time; sometimes just one word at a time.

Never before had I realized the very specialized language we speak in church.

Next Sunday, as you listen to the sermon or the discussion in class, try to listen with an outsider's ear. Would you understand what was being said?

Or would it be a foreign language to you?

Say What?

It was time to go to bed, so my husband and I headed for the bedroom, but he left the light on beside his chair. I turned my light off and then turned his off for him.

As I sat down on my side of the bed, my husband remarked about it taking me so long to get to bed. I explained I had many things to do, including turning off his light for him. That's when it all began.

He assured me he had, indeed, turned his own light off. I, of course, knew that he hadn't. We finally gave it up and went to sleep.

The very next night, as I was getting in bed, my husband pointed to the lamp on the nightstand by his side of the bed and said, "I've made sure to turn my own light off tonight." I cracked up laughing. I understood immediately that on the previous night we had been talking about two different lights. The poor man was almost convinced that I really had turned his bedside lamp off for him.

My middle daughter, Lyn, loved to climb. One of her delights was to climb the door frame and drop on her unsuspecting little sister, Rene', as she passed through the door. One day, just after she completed a drop, I said, "I don't ever want to see you do that again".

An hour later, from another room, I heard Rene' howling in anger. Sure enough, the body bomb had dropped on her. I looked Lyn in the eye and asked, "What did I just tell you?"

Quickly she responded, "That you didn't ever want to see me do that again. And you didn't."

One time my sister had a very bad cold, so she went to bed prepared to blow her nose if needed; handkerchief in place. However, she failed to notify her husband of this. They got settled in bed, she curled up to his back and then, without moving, she blew her nose as hard as she could. Her husband jumped out of bed, quite sure his back was covered with, well you know. Only after he calmed down did he see the handkerchief in her hand.

My husband and I took a trip by car and had to wait while a wreck was being cleared from the highway in front of us. When we got home, our granddaughter asked about our trip. One of the things we shared with her was that there was a wreck and we just sat on the road and waited while it was being taken care of. We told her since we were on vacation, we got out our books and a snack and sat there reading.

Her question: "But what did you do with your car?"

One day my cell phone rang and a man's voice I did not recognize was on the other end. I asked, "Who is this?" Then began a comedy routine.

"This is your son".

"I have a son? What would my son's name be?"

"Adam".

A pregnant pause … "Are you my mother?" And then a click.

I have no sons.

The World from Alta's View

In 1897 the New York Sun newspaper ran the famous editorial, "Yes, Virginia, there is a Santa Claus". The mode of transportation was horses. Earlier that year, in a town called Golden, a baby girl was born and given the name of Alta Vilotta.

As Alta grew, the world around her was changing. A new bicycle race called the Tour de France was announced. A lot of firsts; the first regular transatlantic radio broadcast between the United States and England, the first automobile trip across the United States from San Francisco to New York on dirt roads covered with crushed rock and the Ford Motor Co. sold its first Model A car. In 1903, at a place called Kittyhawk, the Wright brothers made history flying in the air for six minutes.

Alta witnessed Halley's Comet as it approached the sun in 1910.

In Alta's teen years, she married. Their first child, Agnes, was born in 1916 followed quickly in succession by twin daughters Jewett and Jewell (one of whom died in infancy) and sister Myrle.

The marriage didn't last, leaving Alta with three small children. Two suitors showed up, one who brought candy to the children and one who brought candy to Alta and said, "Don't let the children see this." She married the one who cared about the children.

Alta learned to drive. Traveling in a touring car, she turned a corner too soon and ended up in the ditch, tossing her daughters from the back seat. She vowed to never drive again…and she didn't.

In 1925, Mussolini took over power in Italy, Al Jolson premiered in New York and Babe Ruth was rushed to the hospital for ulcer surgery. In Kansas, Alta gave birth to a son and named him Bobby.

The Ku Klux Klan was strong in Kansas, with over 40,000 members. William Allen White, angered by the organization, could not sit idly by, so he ran for Governor of Kansas; going after the KKK.

Another little girl, Joan, was soon added to Alta's burgeoning family. Tragedy struck again when her next baby, Lila Lee, did not survive more than a few months.

Hitler began the production of Volkswagens and the first flight of the Hindenburg occurred in 1936. Margaret Mitchell wrote "Gone With the Wind" and the first edition of Life magazine was published. King Edward VIII abdicated his throne to marry the commoner Mrs. Wallis Simpson. Alta gave birth to another boy, naming him Carl.

World War II was in progress, a Japanese submarine was discovered in the mouth of the Columbia River in Oregon, gasoline was rationed in the United States and Mary Frank went into hiding with her family in 1942. In Emporia, Kansas, Alta gave birth to another little girl. Her husband wanted to name the baby Lois Pauline. However, he died within hours of the baby's birth and the name Lois Joy was written on the birth certificate.

President Truman gave the OK to build the hydrogen bomb in 1950. The Dick Tracy TV show sparked an uproar concerning the violence on the show. Bell Laboratories created the telephone answering machine and Paul Harvey began his national radio broadcast.

Alta's ice box was replaced with an electric refrigerator and a party line telephone was installed in her home. She no longer used a washboard for her laundry, but now had a Maytag wringer washer.

By 1960, USSR had launched Sputnik 5 with two dogs inside. They were recovered … the first living organisms to return from space. In the United States, the Mercury-Redstone 1 test launch failed. We were behind in the space race. In Washington D.C., John F. Kennedy was elected our first Roman Catholic president.

By 1961 Alan Shepard had flown in the United States' first suborbital flight and by 1963 Gordon Cooper was launched into space, becoming the first human to sleep in space. It was July of 1969 when Neil Armstrong took his moon walk. Alta told anyone who would listen that it was all staged at some movie set somewhere.

The return of Halley's Comet occurred in 1985, once again witnessed by Alta. Within a few months, Alta's leg was amputated, removing her only form of transportation. She didn't make it.

In Alta's seasons of life she had seen tremendous changes in the world.

Oh My, What a Year

What a question. Did I know anyone who would like a free round trip ticket to Los Angeles for five days at New Years? Yes, since I had two daughters living there. One string was attached. I had to travel as B. Smith. The owner of the ticket was taking his office staff to LA for the holiday and B. Smith could not go. In 1986, identification was not checked against the name on the ticket.

That's how I ended up sitting on the curb of Main Street in Disneyland. My daughter and I had watched the holiday parade, and now just sat and talked. Little did I know she had a surprise growing inside her.

New Year's Day, my other daughter took me to the park where the floats from the Tournament of Roses Parade were parked. We got up close and personal, able to see all the tiny details that compose the picture on the float. Impressive.

Then B. Smith returned home.

A friend of ours had asked my husband several times if he would re-locate to Tri-Cities, Washington. to start a business. In March, standing in my kitchen in Boise, I felt very sure that we were to make that move. Within two months, my husband was living 300 miles away. I stayed at my job to help train my replacement, who was pregnant. They would let me move away if I promised to return and fill in after she had her baby. I agreed.

July was moving time. I already had a job awaiting me, secured for me by my now ex-boss. Within days of the move, the promised job fell apart. Our new business was still in the baby stages, and money was very tight.

That's when my husband's teenage daughter decided to come live with us. We had been empty nesters for a year and liked it. Two weeks after her arrival, I received a late-night phone call that my youngest daughter had gone into premature labor and been admitted to a hospital in Canada. Within days my first grandchild was born, weighing 2 lbs. 11 oz. While I was still reeling from the speed of my life, my brother called to say our mother had been admitted to a hospital in Kansas. She had an open ulcer on her leg. At the age of 89, she had just decided to live with it, not letting anyone know.

I had a grandbaby struggling to live in Canada and a mother struggling for her life in Kansas. I felt torn in two. The baby stabilized and surgery was performed on mother to amputate her leg.

I was called back to work in Boise for the month of October. My grandchild was still in the neonatal critical care unit, but holding her own. Mother seemed to be was improving and the doctor was talking about her release from the hospital.

Mother didn't make it. My boss arranged for my round-trip flight from Boise to Kansas, making sure I returned quickly.

By November I was back in Washington and my grandchild was ready for her release from the hospital. However, it seemed the young parents were not capable of providing a home for her. I was working four part time jobs to keep us going financially. So my brother and his wife offered to take her. What a mind shift . She was now going to live in Texas.

I couldn't dwell on that long, because my other brother's heart was failing and he needed open heart surgery. He pulled through.

It had been a long, hard year, so we decided to end the year by skiing at Anthony Lakes in Oregon. The day was almost over and I had decided that I didn't want to ski any more. But I acquiesced to the begging and said, "OK, one more run." That's when I was broadsided. I heard my knee pop, my gloves were ripped from my hands and I lay on the ground in pain, with the teenage girl who had run over me dancing all around me repeatedly asking "Are you OK?" No, I wasn't.

I finished the year on crutches.

Even with the eventful year, I never lost my firm belief that we were supposed to make that move to Washington. But I was very glad when 1986 came to an end.

Title: Time With the Healer

A sudden need for major surgery sent my life spiraling. Who would take care of my kids? What would I do for money with six weeks off work? I had no family I could turn to, and my husband had been gone for three years. I was used to handling crisis on my own. But I had never had major surgery and the thought of it caused my stress level to shoot off the Richter scale.

Now the night before surgery had arrived. Wearing a mask of assurance that all was well, I deposited my three children at three different homes, where they would stay until I was released from the hospital.

It was a lonely night. My efforts to keep my imagination under control were ineffective. What would happen to the kids if I died? The long night slowly crept toward the time to go to the hospital. I drove through the darkness, wondering how I was going to make it.

I was greeted with a no-nonsense lady who just wanted the facts. My identification bracelet was attached to my wrist, my clothes and belongings removed from my possession and my new lodging was a two-bed room, with the other bed empty. I didn't know whether to laugh or cry. Did I want company or not?

My feet dangled from the bed and my open-air gown caused a draft in the back. I waited for the procedure to begin. A nurse stuck a thermometer in my mouth and placed her fingers on my pulse. Some notes were written on my chart and then she placed a different thermometer in my mouth.

My temperature was elevated. The doctor arrived to explain the surgery would have to be postponed for 24 hours until my temperature came down. I might be coming down with something that could complicate the operation.

24 hours? I couldn't wait in this room by myself for 24 hours. "God, please don't do this to me. I've already got enough going on." He didn't respond.

I paced the floor. I stared out the window and paced some more. I glanced at the night stand where I had placed my Bible. Would reading that help? Could I find the words I needed for this moment? It had worked before. I climbed in bed and reached for it.

Not sure where to start, I read the 23rd Psalm. There were some pretty good words in there. He promised to restore my soul. I sure needed that. I didn't care too much about the valley of the shadow of death. Was I going to die? Maybe I needed to find something else.

I flipped to the back of the Bible to the concordance. What did it have to say about worry? Apparently nothing, since that word wasn't listed. How about fear? Yes, that word was there with several verses to look up.

And so began my odyssey. I scrounged in my purse and found some paper and a pen. One verse led to another. Soon I was deep in Bible study and my fear level dropped. It was obvious God cared about me and my situation. Hadn't I known that all along?

Then I discovered Matthew 6:25-34. Words like "do not be anxious for your life…." and "which of you by being anxious can add a single cubit to his life's span?" told me that God knew exactly how I was feeling. Those verses ended with "Therefore, do not be anxious for tomorrow…."

It was as if God had spoken them directly to me.

My spirit lifted as I continued my search. The word anxious was in the concordance, so I had a whole new list of scriptures to look up. Before I knew it, hours had flown by. It was an amazing time. I would read a little and then talk to God a little. He felt so very close.

The day was gone. A nurse came in with a sleeping pill for me. I rejected it. I had something much better than a pill. God was in that room and He would help me sleep. God knew exactly what I needed, and He arranged for me to have it…24 hours with Him. I slept soundly, resting on His promises.

I was not surprised when my temperature was normal the next morning. My illness had been in my spirit, not my body. The Healer had known what medicine I needed and dispensed it.

The Silent Generation

The Silent Generation consists of people born between 1925 and 1945. It was named after me, the silent one. But my personal silent generation extended beyond the 1945 boundary, right on through the Baby Boom Generation and Generation X. By the time I poked my head out of my shell, Generation Y was upon us.

During the 50's, 60's and 70's I was encased in a religious cocoon constructed to protect me from the evil ones. Anyone who didn't attend our church fit that category. That fact makes for awkward moments today when someone talks to me about a song they loved in the 60's. When I tell them I've never heard of it, disbelief floods their face.

"Oh, of course you have. You've just forgotten." So, they sing me a little of it.

"Nope, I've never heard it."

Then the questions begin. "Why…how come…who said you couldn't…and on and on.

When you've missed 30 years of music, hairstyles and fashions, it's difficult to catch up. I don't know what I've missed.

My research tells me that poodle skirts were the rage in the 50's. My classmates wore them, along with the short hair that was in style. But my mother did not believe in cutting hair. Hers hung below her waist when it wasn't braided and twisted into a bun. It would be years before I learned that cutting your hair was not a sin.

One of my awkward moments occurred in 2001, when George Harrison died. George who? I was attending a Toastmasters meeting where other members were discussing his death. Imagine the silence that followed when I asked who he was. The Beatles had definitely been off limits for me. My personal music trainer, my husband, provided song after song of theirs for me, assisting in my Beatles education.

I missed out on so many music styles; Rock and Roll, the Blues, Peter, Paul and Mary. And even though the hairdos changed to a beehive look, my hair remained the same. No beehive for me.

When I married in 1980, my husband was aghast that I knew nothing about Elvis. A video was rented to allow me to see him in action. After watching it, I understood why he was off limits for any member of our church. Such gyrations.

My ex-husband was a minister, and it was against church rules to own a television. Those antennas were the devil's horns. Then history happened. John F. Kennedy was shot. One renegade church member had a television, so the congregation gathered at his house to watch the tragedy unfold.

There was also a war going on in a place called Vietnam. Discussion about that must have been off limits, leaving me safe in my cocoon. Hairstyles went from one extreme to the other. Some wore their hair long and straight, pressing it with an iron. Others wore an Afro. Bras became optional. All this happened outside my frame of reference. Our church did not have to deal with such issues.

We lived in a town in Texas that did not allow people of color to remain within the city limits after dark. That fact was made known to me by over-hearing conversation at church one day about a black man who had tried to stay overnight. How dare he?

Out of everything I missed out on, the subculture called hippies fascinated me the most. They were the exact opposite from me. What would that have been like, to be free? A little piece of my hippie-ness came out when I married in

1980. We were married beside a river. I was barefoot and had a halo of flowers in my hair. Just a tiny piece of catching up.

The first time I saw the movie, Flashdance, I cried so hard I couldn't finish watching it. I cried again the next time…and the next, grieving for the deprivations of my childhood. Tapping my fingers or foot in time to music was just not allowed. Something deep within me longed to be able to move to music like Jennifer Beals.

Now Generation Z has come and gone. Beginning in 2010, our new era is as yet unnamed. But I am no longer left out. I can manipulate my iPhone 4 with the best of them, texting many times a day. Just to make sure I'm keeping up; I've started a blog.

Next up…Twitter.

Topic: Week(s)

So Many Memories

Rain slithers down the window as my husband and I pass slowly through the picturesque countryside. The click, clack of the train combined with snores from a fellow passenger make for a strange syncopation of rhythm.

A little black boy prances down the aisle, stopping to talk to everyone. It's my turn, and he speaks rapidly to me in a foreign language. Suddenly his mother (I assume) looms large in the picture, and from the sound of things, he's in big trouble.

Josef, a man we've just met, leans across the aisle and says, "You have just entered Germany."

At the next town, the train pulls to a stop and shuts down. Josef, who has become our temporary tour guide, explains. "The engines must be turned off so we can change the electric systems to German power."

The train jerks to life and we head for Cologne where we need to change trains to reach our final destination, Dusseldorf, where my husband is attending a meeting.

At the Cologne ticket counter my husband asks, "Sproicken de English?"

"Nien" is the response and they point to the next window.

Tickets purchased, we climb aboard a packed train, finding two seats across from two middle-aged men.

"Sproicken de English?"

"Nien."

"Dusseldorf?"

The men respond with words we don't understand but the heads are nodding in the right direction. This must be the correct train.

At the ticket counter we were told the trip would take about 30 minutes. I keep an eye on my watch. About 27 minutes later we hear the word "Dusseldorf" in the announcement. We start to get up.

In chorus, the two men say, "Nien."

Apparently, we don't get off here, so we sit back down. One man holds up three fingers and says, "minutae." OK, we'll wait three minutes.

The train slows again, we rise, and our protectors allow us to get off.

We spy a taxi and say, "Queens Hotel." As the driver throws our luggage in the trunk, he is muttering about 100 metres. He probably also included some words about crazy Americans. He drives out of the train station, turns the corner and comes to a stop in front of the Queens Hotel.

Our room number is 219. But just to keep us on our toes, the main floor is 0. So, room 219 is really on the third floor. This will be our home for almost a week. After a book, bath and apple pie with ice cream, we enjoy a wonderful night's sleep. Breakfast comes with the room: cold juices, hot drinks, eggs, sausage, breads, potatoes and fruit.

My husband leaves for his meeting. The lady at the front desk (who speaks a little English) shows me how to get to the shopping strip called Konigsallee, which means street of kings. I pass shops, restaurants and sex shops before I arrive at Konigsallee.

I receive a surprise when I follow the signs to the toilette. At the doorway sits a lady, her hand out, expecting money. I hold out my handful of Deustche Marks, she flicks through them, shakes her head and motions for me to go on in.

Back at the hotel that night, my husband decides to try the hot tub. He doesn't stay long. The hot tub contains two couples in only their "skivvies."

The next evening the Rhine River provides the backdrop for us as we dine. I have creamed chicken with corn and beans over a baked potato. Delicious.

His meeting over, my husband and I take a little side trip to the town of Wuppertal to visit Helmut, a friend of a friend. He meets us at the train and gives us a running commentary on everything as we pass. He points out a monorail system, the only system like that in the world, called a people mover. Each day, 70,000 people use it to go back and forth to work. It has been in operation for almost 100 years and never had an accident until the week before we came. Now it's closed.

When our visit is over, Helmut offers to take us back to Dusseldorf, so we pile in his van. On the highway, Helmut drives faster and faster (and we have no seat belts). I can see the speedometer. We are going 180 kilometers, flying down the autobahn.

"How fast is that?"

He grins. "Over 100 mph."

So little time…so many memories…all over way too soon.

24 Hours

As I thought about how much time is consumed watching television, my thoughts turned to Mother Teresa. Did she ever watch television? So I did some research on her.

In a typical day, 6:00 a.m. was the beginning of her public time, starting with attending mass. From 7:00 a.m. to 1:00 p.m. she was busy fulfilling her mission; going to different houses and meeting with people. After returning to the house where she lived, she had various meeting set up with other people. She also assisted people in various other ways, overseeing the operations.

Afternoon was when she had time for private prayer and then would meet with the sisters. That flowed into an open prayer service that others could attend. But usually from about 1:00 p.m. to 4:00 p.m. the sisters had a time of renewal. A lot of the work was grueling, so they needed re-energizing. After 4:00 p.m. the meetings, visiting people and assisting others began again, carrying on into the evening. No mention of television.

Not exactly a typical day for me.

I believe the television has created an imbalance in our lives. I've been in homes where there is a television in every room. I know people who watch one while they cook and eat. There is a t.v. in the bathroom and one in the bedroom. Some people use television as sort of a babysitter, placing their children in front of it for hours at a time. Others use it to lull them to sleep and they leave it on all night.

Television prevents communication. When a person's eyes are looking at the t.v., you aren't making contact. Children (and spouses) are the big losers here. If they want family time, then they need to sit where the television is.

Don't get me wrong. I watch television. But I try to pick and choose carefully what I want to see and hear. When I weigh the good I accomplish in my life against how many hours I watch television, the good is the loser.

I've been a NASCAR fan for years. The races are usually on Sunday, so I record them and watch when we get home from church. But in the past year or two, I've had this little conviction niggling at me. We could go out to breakfast with someone from church; perhaps make new friends or help someone who needs a listening ear. Just how important is NASCAR in the face of that?

I'm still in the process of figuring out where God wants my line to be. But when I add up the hours that I read my Bible and pray, and compare that to the hours I sit in front of a television, it's not a good feeling.

Mother Teresa set a very high bar.

We are each given 24 hours. To stay healthy, we should sleep for eight of those hours. That leaves us 16. If we work eight hours a day, we are down to a balance of eight. I try to exercise for one of those hours. My goal is to stay healthy physically.

That leaves seven hours to juggle paying bills, taking care of children (and husband) housework, grocery shopping, cooking, eating, and the list goes on. We are tired, sit down and turn on the television.

And now I'm back to the niggling conviction. If I have set aside one hour for exercise, where is my one hour (minimum) with God? Don't I desire to stay healthy spiritually? Of course I do. So now what?

How much of your 24-hour bucket is taken up by watching television? I'm just askin'.

Giver or Receiver

I squirmed as Bob placed the purchases from the grocery cart onto the conveyor belt. As his hand brought forth two boxes of Tampax, I looked away, overwhelmed with embarrassment. This man was my employer. I babysat for him and his wife, Merilyn. And now he was buying me feminine hygiene supplies.

I first met Bob and Merilyn in a Sunday school class I joined after moving to their town. It didn't take many Sundays for me to realize that Merilyn was a professor at the college across the street from where I lived. As I garnered enough courage to actually speak up in class, she determined my need for income.

That is how I became their babysitter. Many days, as I left for home, she would give me a bag of groceries. But on this day the conversation had gone like this.

"So, Lois, do you have food to eat at home?"

"Sure, we are doing OK."

"We know you've just come through a very hard time and have no income. Would you let us help you?"

"No, we will be just fine. But thanks."

"OK, you just aren't getting it. We want to help. We have the means to help. God wants us to help. But your pride is not going to let us? You are depriving us from receiving a blessing."

Pride? I didn't know I had any left. But, yes, it was pride that I didn't want them to take me to the store and buy stuff for me. I was on my own and I was determined to make it. But Merilyn wasn't through.

"Sometimes in life we are the giver and sometimes the receiver. When you get on your feet, you can pass it on and help someone else. Wouldn't you like to do that?"

"Yes, right after I paid you back."

"So, you would let us have just a temporary blessing and then take it away?"

I gave in.

Merilyn stayed home with the kids so she could start dinner and sent Bob to the store with me. At the front of the store, he retrieved a cart and said, "Lois, we are just going to go up and down the aisles and you put what you need in the cart. OK?"

Going down the first aisle, I put a gallon of milk in the cart and kept walking, reaching for a dozen eggs. When I turned to place the eggs in the cart, Bob had returned to the beginning of the aisle. He motioned for me to come to him. I obeyed; carton of eggs in my hand.

"Ok, we can do this the easy way or the hard way. When we get to the other side of the store, I expect this cart to be so full you can't put anything else in it. Now, do you want to pick what goes in, or do you want me to pick for you? You will probably get some things you don't need or don't want, but the cart will be full. Which is it?"

I put stuff in.

I learned a HUGE lesson that day. The Bible says "It is more blessed to give than to receive." If we don't allow someone to give, we block their blessing. As my life improved, I began the process of giving. Oh, it wasn't much, but I received a blessing. And when the receiver began to talk of repaying, I just quoted Bob.

Bob kept giving to the end. Merilyn needed a kidney to survive. Bob was a match, but too heavy for the surgery. He quickly lost down to a healthy weight and gave his wife a kidney. But there were complications for Bob.

He didn't make it.

Maybe today you can be the giver. But maybe someone else needs to be the giver and you need to learn to be the receiver. Pride is not a good thing and it blocks the channel of blessing.

Musician Extraordinaire

It all started with a scratched and dented cornet. But at the age of eleven and with no money of his own, that horn was like a precious treasure to him. As he played in the Salvation Army Band, he held the cornet high and blew with pride, a budding musician.

By the time he reached high school, he had moved on to a bigger and better instrument, a euphonium, becoming Principal Euphonium player with the Kansas All-State High School Band. The battered cornet now had a place of honor on a shelf in the small area he called his room.

His graduation from high school was the springboard to get him away from the poverty and oppressed religious life that had been forced upon him. The Navy offered a way of escape and he took it. Four years of his life were dedicated to playing his euphonium as a U. S. Navy Musician.

Now with a wife and child he chose Colorado as his new home, where he became Principal/Solo Euphonium with the Colorado State University

Symphonic Wind Ensemble, and Principal Trombone with the CSU Symphony Orchestra.

His second child was due any day when he received a phone call from the Navy. He had been selected to audition for a spot in the Naval Academy Band and he had to travel to Maryland to perform. Placing his little family in the car, he drove through the night to the town in Kansas where he had grown up, left his son and very pregnant wife there with her aunt, picking up his sister and her finance'. After a fast-paced trip across the United States, he arrived in the Annapolis area in time to shave, clean up and put on a suit in a filling station's bathroom.

He passed the audition.

He drove quickly back to Kansas, arriving in time for the birth of his daughter. Within days the family's residence was no longer Colorado, but Maryland.

With the U. S. Naval Academy Band, he was the Principal/Solo Euphonium. He also played trombone with the big band. Within a few years, he became an Assistant Director, U. S. Navy Academy Band, and then Director, U. S. Navy Band, CNATRA. He retired after 20 years.

But he wasn't through with music.

He became Manager, North American Region Four for Boosey & Hawkes of London, England. They were the manufacturer and distributor of fine musical instruments. He held this position for another 20 years, until he again retired.

He taught Low Brass at Colorado State University, Pueblo, until he retired again. Apparently, he never quite understood the meaning of the word retirement. And so, he taught euphonium, trombone and tuba at the University of Southern Colorado while performing and teaching as an Artist/Clinician for Besson Brasses.

Other accomplishments include performing with the Fountain Creek Brass Band, the Colorado Brass Band, the Chamber Orchestra of the Springs, and the Colorado Wind Ensemble. He's past member of the Texas Wind Symphony, the Dallas Tuba/Euphonium Quartet and Ensemble, the Florida Symphonic Band, the Fort Worth Concert Band, the Charlotte Symphony, the Venice Symphony, the Corpus Christi Concert Band, the Rocky Mountain Brassworks, the Little London Winds, the Pueblo Symphony and the Pikes Peak Philharmonic.

He has worked with the Colorado Springs Philharmonic, the Denver Municipal Band, the Corpus Christi Symphony, the Florida West Coast Symphony and the Heidelberg, Germany Municipal Band.

Along the way he has appeared with the Four Tops, Patti Page, Holiday on Ice, Joni Mitchell, the Jimmy Dorsey Orchestra, the Bob Crosby Band, Clark Terry, Frank Rosolino, Urbie Green, Al Hirt, Monty Alexander, Marian McPartland, Frank Sinatra and many other notable entertainers.

And how, you ask, do I know so much about this musician?

He is my brother. I grew up listening to his music, with or without an instrument. I've never heard anyone who could whistle like he can. Music and rhythm poured from him no matter what we were doing. If we were eating, his fork was keeping time to the song in his head.

Traveling by car across country, he never missed his practice time. A campground would become a concert hall, people would gather round and he would perform away; enjoying every minute, I might add.

Briefly I was his neighbor in Maryland. That was the only time in my life I got to see him in his uniform and hear his performance. I tried not to yell too loudly…not proud or anything.

Banishing the Ogre

She lived with fear, all day and every night. Fear of the known. There was an ogre that was out to get her, who watched her every move. She never knew just when it might appear, but she had to stay ready.

The fight or flight syndrome never left her.

Morning light, and before she even opened her eyes, she could feel its presence. As she readied herself for the day, each movement required her undivided focus. Was she walking too heavily across the floor? If the family living downstairs complained about her noise, there would be consequences.

Eyes cast downward; she silently ate the oatmeal and burnt toast placed in front of her. More silence as she gathered her school books and moved cautiously toward the door. So far, so good. But the day stretched out before her, long and tiring. There would be no rest this day, or any day, for her exhausted spirit. The ogre was everywhere, even at school.

She observed the other kids, laughing and shoving, talking and playing games. Apparently they didn't care they were being watched. What would that feel like…to be unafraid of punishment? As that thought flitted through her mind, she frantically glanced around. Where was it?

Was it waiting until school was over to show itself?

Her steps were slow and methodical as she headed home. Would it be tonight…or would she be safe one more day? The relentless tension in her body became even more severe the closer she got; her stomach in painful spasms. Evenings were the very hardest.

Constantly trying to be perfect was utterly exhausting.

Carefully she placed her schoolbooks on the table, their one and only table, where she would have to do her homework. But she hadn't been cautious enough.

"It's a sin to be upset and bang your books on the table like that. You'll have to go to the altar on Sunday and confess that sin." The words or else hung in the air.

When would the ogre strike?

Bedtime, and she eased herself onto her side of the bed. The other side was reserved for her mother as they shared their one and only bed. But sleep was elusive and restless. The ever-present ogre waited for her to slip up even now.

Was there no way to banish the ogre?

Burnout

I had so much love to give, and that nine-year old little girl in foster care was so needy, I had to do something. Given the fact that child was my grand-daughter made my actions even a higher priority.

So, the process began to obtain temporary custody.

Twelve months passed, thousands of dollars flowed, before the courts pronounced it a done deal. I now had my chance to restore Marie's spirit. But the scenario in my head of how it would go and the actuality of what really occurred were worlds apart.

Marie had no off button.

Mealtimes and there seemed to be a spring in her chair.

"I have to go to the bathroom. No, I really have to go. Ok, I'll just pee in my chair then."

She was allowed to go. Before the next meal, she was sent to the bathroom before she sat down. But eating at the table until she was through with the meal was just not possible. She chewed as she paced. She chewed as she banged the silverware on the plate. She chewed as she talked non-stop.

It was time for the annual house cleaning, with ladies hired to help.

"What do you want us to do with all the pills under the chair in the family room?"

Every vitamin I had given her was under the chair.

Her mind never stopped.

"What would happen if, and the sentence would be completed with a plane crashed into this house…I walked down the street and you never saw me again… I put aluminum foil in the microwave?

She tried the last one, placing a ball of foil in the microwave and enjoying the sparks, but was caught in time, before the fire started; causing her great disappointment.

The walls were a great canvas for her artistry, sometimes using fecal matter instead of markers.

There was no rest for the weary.

Nighttime brought no relief. Marie slept in bits and pieces. The rest of the night was time to re-arrange her room, strip her bed, make several trips to the bathroom and turn lights on all over the house.

She had to be watched every minute, which made it difficult to take a shower. She couldn't be trusted to be in the house for those brief moments, but would she stay in the yard while I bathed?

I never knew.

There were the calls from school. "You better come. Marie is trying to break the school windows."

I found her in the Principal's office, with the school counselor.

"Marie, what's going on?"

"They said I touched the rope and I didn't. They won't believe me."

She had been playing tetherball, the rope had wrapped around her arm, and she had been called out because she touched the rope.

I understood immediately. She hadn't touched the rope, it touched her.

I explained to the counselor what needed to be said next time, "the rope touched you", and she would not react.

One day the phone rang, and the caller ID told me the incoming call was from the Kennewick Police Department. Instantly I wondered what Marie had done now.

"We have Marie here at the Police Station. Would you please come down?"

Did I have a choice?

That morning, in the newspaper, there had been an article about a bomb that had been placed in a trash barrel at Marie's school. I watched as she read the story. Later, at school, the police visited each room to ask if anyone knew anything about the bomb. Marie's hand went up. She knew all about it.

Again, the question had been worded incorrectly for her. She had nothing to do with the bomb, but it took me several hours to convince the police of that fact.

I longed for just one night of unbroken sleep; for just a few hours when I could let down my guard and not be on alert.

Back in court for another hearing, with me on the witness stand. The Judge asked, "Why did you go for just temporary custody?" I looked him straight in the eye and said, "Because I want to be her grandmother."

With a slight nod of his head, I knew he understood.

Marie's aunt moved to our town to establish residency and seek permanent custody. Help was on the way…and then I could rest.

The First Step is the Hardest

He was gone, her husband of 13 years. Like a robot, she moved through her days and nights. The church she had devoted her life to kicked her out because he left.

She was on her own.

Winter came, and in Nebraska winters were brutal. Learning to put chains on the tires seemed impossible, but she did it. Since the only job she could find was selling Avon, she needed to be able to traverse the slippery hills. But she and the three children could not subsist on Avon income alone.

Slowly she sold the furniture, took in ironings and became a seamstress for others. Her future was bleak.

For two years she struggled to keep their heads above water. She needed a new beginning. But that would require more courage than she had; to climb in a car, drive to a new place with her children and begin again.

Then came the day, with help from a brother's counsel, she reached the decision she had endured enough. Life had to get better. It would take planning;

something for which she had no practice. The neighbors across the street were in constant contact with the children's father, even though he lived in another state. His threat had been "If you try anything, I will get you." She believed him.

And so the planning began. More furniture was sold. Soon the house was almost empty. The upcoming move required money she didn't have; so, the saving began with scrimping on essentials. Her car was old and falling apart, but she had no other options.

The lawyer she consulted regarding the legality of moving had only confused the issue.

"Legally, you are required to stay in this state. But since he is no longer residing here, you aren't actually taking the children away from him. I advise you to move. But if it comes to court, I will deny saying that."

Swell.

The time drew near. Even the children knew nothing of the plan. It was safer that way. Her first destination was a town where her niece had made arrangements for them to stay overnight with a family until they could get to their new home.

As bedtime neared, the children were informed to pack what they could in a few suitcases. They were leaving this life. Anger, tears, begging and hatred were directed at her. But she knew something they didn't. Life could be better.

As the sky darkened, they climbed in the car and left that house for the last time. Per the instructions from the lawyer, they headed straight south to cross the state line. Two days later they arrived at their final destination. The car still had four tires and an engine that worked. It took only another 24 hours for that to no longer be true. But they had made it.

Welfare wouldn't take them; giving her the counsel to get in the car and go back. She had come this far. Going back was not an option. She fought and won. It was mortifying, but she was on Welfare and would have some food and money. Their housing was a one-bedroom apartment. Determined that they each have their own bed, she purchased two bunk beds.

She still struggled. But there was a light at the end of this tunnel, so she labored on. Acquiring a job, the one-bedroom apartment became a two-bedroom duplex, with the children drawing straws to see who was stuck with sleeping in the same room as mom. Their next move was to a house, with each of them having their own room.

Life was getting better.

There was still anger and rebellion. Uprooting the children had been a difficult decision, one they might never understand. Yet she knew in her heart it had been the right one.

They were free here; free to breathe and live and grow.

What is that Sound

My world was full of sound. As I walked on the treadmill, Chuck Swindoll's voice came through my headset, expounding on the word of God. The gym's radio was doing what it does best, blaring obnoxious music if you can call it that. To my right, two treadmills over, were two ladies talking and laughing. From the weight room I heard the clank of free weights and then the thud as they were dropped to the floor.

Yet I could hear humming.

To my left, two treadmills over, a lady walked steadily holding on to the machine, eyes closed and softly humming. I knew the song. Amazed I could hear her above all the other noise, I forgot Chuck as I listened to song after song. She was in her own world; totally unaware she was having any affect on me.

That's a perfect example of how I desire my Christ-like life to be.

Our world is so full of chaos, noise and activity, that the soft sound of a Christ-like spirit is difficult to hear. Some of us blare our song like the obnoxious music from the radio. Others laugh and talk about surface things, never really saying anything important. There are those focused only on building themselves up. They go through life lifting the weights of Bible study and more Bible study, that they never really touch the life of another.

And then there is the person who loves God and others, who softly hums in the background a song about being real and caring about people. That's who I strive to be.

I Am Woman

Women used to know exactly what role was expected of them. They played with dolls as children so they could grow up and become mothers and have children. Simple, wasn't it?

It's not so simple anymore.

Our daughter was here for a visit. As she described her life to me, I became exhausted. She never stops. Two children, ages 4 and 8. Gymnastics and baseball. Soccer and ballet.

I turned to Google and typed in "Super Mom Syndrome", not even knowing if there would be anything. I could write a book with the information available on this syndrome. Several people have.

Just being an ordinary, stay-at-home mom is not acceptable.

It's much simpler to just have your role as a mother laid out for you. I've been there. Keep them fed and clean. Make them behave. Get them to school on time. And if they get out of line, it's your fault. You go to bed night after night feeling unfulfilled and a failure.

For the mother of today it is complicated, but much more rewarding. The mother grows along with the child, both before and after birth. She sees each child as an individual and treats them differently in discipline and play. There is no "One size fits all".

It all depends on what you want for your child.

After my first husband left, my three daughters and I lived in two rooms. We ate from a card table. We slept in bunk beds. But my kids look back on those days as some of the best days of their lives. We played games, took walks, made up stories and laughed a lot. They didn't know we were poor.

The atmosphere in those two rooms was up to me. I was strong. I was invincible. I was woman.

Today's mothers are even fighting in a war. That has put a whole new spin on motherhood. Sometimes it's the dad who stays home and kisses the soldier goodbye.

I remember buying a set of black plastic dishes once, after I saw an ad on television where they actually put a blowtorch to them, and they emerged unscathed. Exactly one week after I bought them, one of the kids brought a dinner plate to me with a large crack in it. When I asked what happened, she said it hit a tree.

I don't want to talk about it. But I'm still woman.

English as a Second Language

English was definitely the second language.

We handed the piece of paper to our taxi driver on which was written our desired destination. In the words that came out of his mouth, we only recognized one…kilometers. My husband pointed to the trunk, nodded his head and indicated we wanted our luggage to be placed there. With a look of puzzlement on his face, the taxi driver complied. We climbed in; he drove out of the train depot, turned left and pulled to a stop.

We had reached our destination.

The next segment of our journey involved going from Germany to Switzerland. Instructions given us were to get off the train in Basel in order to change trains. Signs flashed by the train window and soon we saw the word announcing "Basel Bnd Banhof".

So we got off.

Imagine our surprise when it wasn't an actual train station. There are two "Basel" stops, one in Germany and one in Switzerland. We had gotten off in

Germany. The Swiss train station…with all the connecting trains…was up the tracks several miles. Luckily, another train would be by in a few hours.

In Liechtenstein, no menus were in English. We did notice repetition of a phrase, "pommes frites". With much pointing and movement of hands, the waitress understood we wanted to know what that was. She thought for a moment and then said, "McDonalds".

French fries.

Still in Liechtenstein…different restaurant…the word schinken appeared several times. Again with pointing and hand movements, the waitress understood we wanted to know what that was. After many words and gestures, she proceeded to oink like a pig.

Ham.

It was imperative that I eat no nuts, so I traveled prepared with the phrase "Nien Nusse" on my lips. Apparently it worked. I suffered no reactions.

Connections

The highway was his playground. He rode his sleek, yellow motorcycle through the twisties on Dooley Mountain…turned around and split the air around curve after curve going the other way. He experienced the top of Bear Tooth Mountain in July, with snow on the roadside. He survived a night in a tent in Gillette, Wyoming with the wind, hail and rain so severe motorcycles were on their side the next morning.

He did it all with a huge grin on his face. He loved it.

Though the highway had been his playground, it was no longer. His life took a devastating turn. Now his world consisted of a bed for 18 hours a day, with short trips to the big chair in the family room…catching a nap or two there.

He was outliving his expiration date.

Flowers arrive on a regular basis. Cards express the love of others. And food… even though he says most foods taste like burnt cardboard (when did he ever eat that?)…is delivered to the door. Friends hear that he can taste strawberry milk-shakes. Sometimes we have a backup in the refrigerator as shakes are dropped by for him. Homemade French onion soup delights him. The freezer contains several servings in small meal size containers available when he is ready.

But most of all…friends. Friends who care enough to take time out of their day to come, sit and chat. For a brief time each day, his world expands. He laughs. He listens to their stories and then tells his own.

He connects.